THE SILENCE BETWEEN THEM

THE SILENCE BETWEEN THEM

GEORGINA ROWAN

Chapter One

The breakfast room at Fenleigh House faced east, which meant that on clear mornings, light fell across the table in long, pale bands. Isobel had learned to position herself just outside the brightest of these, where she could read without squinting but remain close enough to the window to feel something like warmth.

Her husband sat at the head of the table, as he did every morning. He was reading correspondence. He had been reading correspondence for the better part of an hour, occasionally making small notations in the margins with a pencil he kept beside his plate. His tea had gone cold. He had not noticed.

Isobel noticed. She noticed most things about Alastair, the way he held his shoulders when he was displeased with something he had read, the particular stillness of his hands when he was thinking, the fact that he took his eggs coddled but rarely finished them. She had been his wife for three years. She had learned him the way one learns the patterns of a house, thoroughly, and out of necessity.

He had not learned her at all.

This was not a complaint. Isobel did not allow herself complaints, not even in the privacy of her own mind. It was simply an observation, made with the same detachment she might use to note that the silver wanted polishing or that the weather had turned.

The footman entered with fresh toast. He moved silently, as all the Fenleigh servants did, trained to efficiency and invisibility. Isobel watched him place the rack on the table, adjust its position slightly, and withdraw without a word. She wondered, not for the first time, whether the servants saw her as one of their own. Another function in the great machine of the household. Another person whose primary virtue was not being noticed.

"I shall be in the study until noon," Alastair said, not looking up. "There is a matter with the eastern tenants that requires attention."

"Of course," Isobel said.

He folded the letter he had been reading and set it aside. For a moment, his gaze moved in her direction. Not quite to her face, but somewhere near her left shoulder. "Is there anything you require?"

The question was perfunctory. She understood that. It was the sort of question a good host might ask a guest, or a steward might ask of a new servant. It required a specific kind of answer, brief, undemanding, resolved.

"No, thank you," she said. "I have letters to write this morning."

"Very good."

He rose, inclined his head in what might have been acknowledgment, and left the room. His footsteps faded down the corridor, measured, unhurried, certain of their destination.

Isobel remained at the table. The light had shifted; now it fell across her hands, which were folded in her lap. She looked at them for a moment, at the thin gold band on her fourth finger, at the neat, clean nails her mother had always insisted upon. *A lady's hands tell the world what sort of woman she is*, her mother had said. *Keep them still. Keep them soft. Keep them ready.*

Ready for what, her mother had never specified. Isobel had eventually concluded that the readiness itself was the point.

She did have letters to write. That had not been a lie. Her younger sister, Charlotte, expected correspondence every fortnight, and Isobel's aunt in Bath sent lengthy, meandering accounts of her health that required equally lengthy responses. There was also a note to be sent to the vicar's wife regarding the charity baskets, and another to the housekeeper at the dower house about the roof tiles that needed replacing before winter.

These were her duties, and she performed them well. The household ran smoothly under her management. The servants respected her. The tenants' wives found her pleasant and undemanding. Even Alastair, on the rare occasions when he thought to remark upon such things, had expressed satisfaction with how she conducted herself.

She was, by every measure that mattered, an excellent duchess.

The thought should have brought her comfort. Instead, it settled somewhere in her chest like a stone dropped into still water, heavy, sinking, leaving only the faintest ripple on the surface.

The morning passed in the usual way.

Isobel met with Mrs. Harding at ten o'clock to discuss the week's menus and the state of the household accounts. The housekeeper was a capable woman in her fifties, grey-haired and sharp-eyed, who had served the Vane family since before Alastair's birth. She treated Isobel with precisely calibrated respect, enough to acknowledge her position, not enough to suggest genuine warmth.

"The butcher has raised his prices again, Your Grace," Mrs. Harding reported. "I have written to express our displeasure, but I thought you should be aware."

"Thank you, Mrs. Harding. Perhaps we might consider the butcher in Grantham instead? I understand his reputation is sound."

"I shall make inquiries."

They discussed the linen inventory, the need to hire an additional scullery maid, the state of the chimneys in the east wing. Isobel made notes in her household book, her handwriting precise and regular. She asked questions, offered suggestions, approved expenditures. She performed, in other words, exactly as she was expected to perform.

When the meeting concluded, Mrs. Harding gathered her papers and rose to leave. At the door, she paused.

"Will there be anything else, Your Grace?"

"No, thank you. That will be all."

The housekeeper nodded and withdrew. Isobel sat alone in the morning room, surrounded by the evidence of her competence, the neat columns of figures, the organized lists, the well-maintained household she had built and sustained.

She felt nothing.

Or rather, she felt many things, but none of them had names she was willing to use. There was a hollowness in her chest that had been growing for months, perhaps years. A sense that she was watching her own life from a great distance, observing but not participating. A creeping suspicion that she had somehow ceased to exist as anything more than the sum of her duties.

She pushed the thought away, as she always did, and went to write her letters.

The library at Fenleigh was vast and underused.

Alastair preferred his study for working and rarely read for pleasure. The previous duchess, his mother, had kept her own small collection in her private rooms and had seen no reason to venture into what she called "that cavern of dust." As a result, the library had become, by default, Isobel's domain.

She came here most afternoons when her duties permitted. She had discovered, early in her marriage, that no one remarked upon her absence if she could be assumed to be somewhere respectable. The library was respectable. It was also quiet, and private, and lined with books that no one but her ever touched.

Today she selected a volume of essays she had been working through slowly, a collection of meditations on natural philosophy that would have horrified her mother. *Unwomanly*, her mother would have said. *Unbecoming.* Her mother believed that women who read too much developed nervous complaints and failed to conceive.

Isobel had been reading voraciously for three years and had developed nothing worse than a mild preference for solitude. As for conception, that was a thought she did not allow herself to complete.

She settled into the chair by the window, the one with the worn velvet cushion that held the shape of her body now, and opened the book to where she had left off. The essay concerned the migration patterns of certain seabirds and their remarkable ability to navigate vast distances without any apparent landmark or guide.

It is a matter of instinct, the author proposed. *The bird does not choose its course; the course is written within it, as indelibly as the colour of its feathers or the shape of its wings.*

Isobel considered this. She wondered what it might feel like, to have a direction written so clearly inside oneself. To know, without doubt or deliberation, where one was meant to go.

She had never felt that. Not once.

Her course had always been set by others, by her father, who had arranged the marriage; by her mother, who had prepared her for it; by Alastair, who had accepted her as one might accept a well-made piece of furniture. Useful. Appropriate. Requiring no particular attention once installed.

She read on, losing herself in the author's descriptions of arctic terns and their impossible journeys. The birds flew from pole to pole each year, covering distances that seemed almost mythological. They did not hesitate. They did not question. They simply flew, following the invisible compass that nature had given them.

What must that be like, she wondered. To have such certainty. To never doubt one's direction.

From somewhere in the house, a clock chimed. Two o'clock. In an hour, she would need to dress for calls. The Ashworth ladies were expected, and afterward, there was a matter with Cook about the menu for next week's dinner.

She closed the book, marking her place with a slip of paper. The seabirds would have to wait.

The Ashworth ladies arrived at three o'clock precisely.

Mrs. Ashworth was a stout woman with strong opinions about everything from the state of the roads to the moral character of the lower classes. Her daughter, Miss Lydia Ashworth, was a pale, nervous creature who rarely spoke unless directly addressed. Isobel received them in the drawing room, poured tea, and settled into the familiar rhythm of social performance.

"Such a lovely room," Mrs. Ashworth pronounced, surveying the decor with the air of a general inspecting troops. "You have made some changes since we were last here, I think?"

"New curtains only," Isobel said. "The previous ones had faded."

"Ah yes. I thought I noticed something different. Very tasteful. Very appropriate." Mrs. Ashworth sipped her tea. "And how is the Duke? Well, I trust?"

"Very well, thank you. He is occupied with estate matters at present, but he sends his regards."

This was not strictly true. Alastair had said nothing about the Ashworths or their visit. He had likely forgotten they were coming. But the fiction was expected, and Isobel provided it without hesitation.

"We are all so pleased about Lydia's engagement," Mrs. Ashworth continued, turning to beam at her daughter. "Mr. Thornwood is an excellent young man. The wedding is to be in June."

"How wonderful. Congratulations, Miss Ashworth."

Lydia colored and murmured something inaudible. She looked, Isobel thought, more terrified than pleased. But perhaps that was only nerves. Brides were supposed to be nervous.

"Of course, you must remember your own wedding day," Mrs. Ashworth said, fixing Isobel with a knowing look. "Such a grand affair it was. The whole county talked of nothing else for weeks."

"You are very kind to remember."

"And three years now, is it? How time flies." Mrs. Ashworth's expression shifted subtly, taking on the particular quality of a woman about to venture into delicate territory. "I wonder if we might soon hear happy news?"

Isobel's hands remained steady on her teacup. She had fielded this question before, from Mrs. Ashworth and others. She had prepared answers, smooth and deflecting, that revealed nothing.

"Such things are in God's hands," she said.

"Indeed, indeed. Though sometimes these matters require patience, do they not? My own mother waited nearly five years for her first, and then had six in as many years after that. These things happen when they are meant to."

"I am sure you are right."

The conversation moved on to other topics, the weather, the state of the parish school, the latest scandal involving a neighboring family. Isobel listened and responded and performed her role with the ease of long practice. She was pleasant. She was gracious. She was everything a duchess ought to be.

Inside, she was screaming.

The Ashworths departed at half past four, and Isobel found herself alone in the drawing room.

The light was fading now, the short winter afternoon already giving way to dusk. A maid appeared to clear the tea things, moving with the quiet efficiency that characterized all the Fenleigh servants. Isobel watched her work and felt a sudden, irrational urge to speak to her. To say something real. To have a conversation that was not performance.

She said nothing. The maid finished her work and withdrew, and Isobel sat alone with the gathering darkness.

Mrs. Ashworth's question echoed in her mind. *Happy news.* The euphemism for pregnancy, for children, for the one thing a wife was ultimately supposed to provide.

She and Alastair had tried. In the early months of their marriage, when duty demanded it and neither of them expected anything more. The encounters had been brief, uncomfortable, conducted with the lights extinguished and as little fuss as possible. Alastair had performed his role competently, as he performed all his roles, and Isobel had endured.

There had been no children. After the first year, Alastair had stopped coming to her bedchamber. She had felt relief, then guilt for feeling relief, then a strange sort of grief for something she was not sure she had ever wanted.

Now, three years in, the question of heirs had taken on a new urgency. Lady Ashworth was not the only one to inquire. Alastair's aunt had written twice on the subject, her letters growing increasingly pointed. Even Isobel's own mother had raised it, during her last visit, with the particular combination of disappointment and resignation that characterized all her communications with her elder daughter.

Perhaps, her mother had said, *you might consult a physician. There are treatments, I am told. Ways to encourage these matters.*

Isobel had not consulted a physician. She had not done anything. She had simply continued as she was, managing the household, performing her duties, slowly disappearing into the wallpaper.

If there were no children, she sometimes thought, what was she for? What purpose did she serve, beyond the running of a house that could have been run by a competent housekeeper?

She did not know the answer. She was not sure she wanted to find one.

That evening, dinner was served at half past seven, as it always was.

Isobel wore the pale blue silk, the one Alastair had once said suited her colouring. She could not remember when he had said it, or whether he had meant it as a compliment or merely an observation, but she had filed it away regardless. It was one of perhaps a dozen remarks he had made about her appearance in three years of marriage.

They sat at opposite ends of the table, as was proper. The distance between them was roughly twenty feet. Isobel had measured it once, during a particularly long dinner, counting the floorboards under the pretext of examining the carpet for wear.

Twenty feet. A vast gulf of mahogany and candlelight and silence.

"The Ashworth ladies called today," she said, when the soup had been cleared and the fish course laid. It was expected that she would make conversation. She did not enjoy it, but she was skilled at it, which amounted to much the same thing in practice.

"Ah." Alastair glanced up briefly. "And how did you find them?"

"Well, thank you. Mrs. Ashworth sends her regards. She mentioned that her daughter's wedding has been fixed for June."

"Has it." This was not a question. "I suppose we shall be expected to attend."

"I imagine so."

"Very well. You may send our acceptance when the invitation arrives."

"Of course."

The fish was removed. A joint of beef was brought in, carved with precision by the footman and served with roasted vegetables. Isobel ate small, neat bites, chewing carefully, swallowing without haste. She had been trained to eat this way, to make the process as unobtrusive as possible, as if the act of nourishing oneself were somehow indelicate.

Alastair ate with the same methodical efficiency he brought to everything. He did not seem to taste the food so much as process it. When he had finished, he set down his knife and fork with a small, definitive click.

"I may be away next week," he said. "There is business in London that requires my attention. I expect to be gone no more than a fortnight."

"I see." Isobel kept her voice even. "Shall I prepare anything for your journey?"

"My valet will see to it. But I thank you."

He thanked her. It was such a small courtesy, and yet it struck her, as such things sometimes did, with unexpected force. He thanked her as he might thank a servant, politely, distantly, without any real sense that she had offered him anything of herself.

Because she hadn't. She never did. And he never asked.

"I hope your business goes well," she said.

"I expect it shall."

And that was all. The silence stretched between them, vast and familiar, punctuated only by the small sounds of cutlery on porcelain and the distant ticking of the clock in the hall.

Isobel looked at her husband across the twenty feet of table and tried to remember if there had ever been a time when she had felt close to him. If there had ever been a conversation that meant something. A moment of genuine connection.

She could not recall one.

Later, alone in her chambers, Isobel sat at her writing desk and drew out the small leather journal she kept locked in the bottom drawer.

It was a plain thing, bound in brown calfskin, with no gilding or ornamentation. She had purchased it herself, three months into her marriage, from a shop in the village where no one knew her face. The shopkeeper had wrapped it in brown paper without comment, and Isobel had carried it home tucked inside her reticule, feeling like a thief.

She opened it to a fresh page, dipped her pen in ink, and paused.

For a long moment, she simply sat there, the pen hovering above the paper. The candle flickered. Beyond the window, the night was very dark, very still. The house around her was quiet, the servants retired, her husband in his own chambers on the other side of the house.

She was alone. She was always alone.

Then, in her careful, even hand, she wrote,

He is going to London. I did not ask why, and he did not offer. I do not know if he has a mistress there. I do not know if I would mind if he did. I think perhaps I should mind. I think a wife is meant to mind such things. But when I try to find the feeling, jealousy, or hurt, or even curiosity, there is nothing. Only this, a kind of blankness, where something else should be.

I wonder sometimes if the fault is mine. If I am made wrong, somehow. Incomplete. Mother always said I was too quiet, too contained. She said men wanted warmth, and I had none to give.

Perhaps she was right.

Perhaps this is simply what I am.

She paused, considering. Then she continued,

Mrs. Ashworth asked today about children. The question I have come to dread, asked with that particular tone of sympathy that women of her sort have perfected. I gave my usual answer. God's will. Patience. Hope.

I am not sure any of those things are true.

I am not sure I want a child. Not like this. Not in this house, with this husband, in this life that feels less like living and more like waiting for something that will never come.

But what else is there? What else could there be?

I do not know. I cannot imagine.

And perhaps that is the greatest tragedy of all.

She set down the pen, read over what she had written, and felt nothing. Or rather, nothing that could be named. There was something there, beneath the stillness, but it was buried too deep to reach.

She closed the journal, locked it away, and went to bed.

In the morning, Alastair would be at breakfast, reading his correspondence. She would sit in her usual place, just outside the band of light. They would speak of nothing, and everything would continue exactly as it was.

She did not know yet that anything could be different.

But she was beginning, in the quietest and most hidden part of herself, to wonder.

Chapter Two

Alastair departed for London on a Tuesday, in a carriage that had been polished to a high gleam by three footmen and a stable boy.

Isobel stood on the front steps to see him off, as was proper. The morning was grey and damp, threatening rain, and she had brought a shawl but forgotten her gloves. Her fingers were cold, curled at her sides, but she did not tuck them into her sleeves. A duchess did not fidget.

"I shall write if there is any delay," Alastair said. He was already looking past her, toward the carriage, his mind clearly on the journey ahead. He wore his traveling coat, dark grey wool with brass buttons, and carried a leather portfolio under his arm. Everything about him spoke of purpose and destination.

"I hope the roads are kind to you."

"They usually are, this time of year."

He hesitated then. A small pause, barely noticeable, in which something might have been said. Isobel felt herself lean toward it, some instinct responding to the possibility of what? A tender word? A touch? Something that might suggest she would be missed?

But the moment passed. Alastair inclined his head, descended the steps, and climbed into the carriage without looking back. The door closed. The driver gathered the reins. The horses began to move.

Isobel remained on the steps until the carriage had disappeared around the curve of the drive. The rain began, soft and steady, spotting her shawl with dark points of damp. She did not move.

Behind her, Mrs. Harding cleared her throat. "Shall I have tea brought to the morning room, Your Grace?"

"Yes," Isobel said. "That would be well."

She turned and went inside. The house swallowed her, as it always did, and the day continued.

The house felt different with Alastair gone.

Not better, exactly. Not worse. Simply looser, somehow. As if it had been holding its breath and could now exhale. The servants moved through the corridors with a slightly different rhythm, and there was more laughter from the kitchens than usual. Even the light seemed to fall differently through the windows, though Isobel knew this was fancy, nothing more.

She had grown accustomed to his absences. In the first year of their marriage, she had dreaded them, not because she missed him, precisely, but because she did not know how to miss him and felt she ought to. She would wander the halls, feeling the emptiness of the house like an accusation. *A good wife would feel his absence keenly. A good wife would count the days.*

Isobel counted nothing. The days passed, indistinguishable from one another, and when Alastair returned, she felt only a slight tightening, as if a corset she had momentarily loosened was being laced up again.

Now, three years in, she had learned to move through his absences like water through familiar channels. There were still the morning consultations with Mrs. Harding, still the afternoon calls and the charity work and the letters that required answering. The structure of her days remained intact. Only the constraint of his presence was lifted.

On the first morning alone, she lingered at breakfast.

This was a small rebellion, but a rebellion nonetheless. When Alastair was home, meals began and ended at precisely appointed times. Breakfast at eight. Luncheon at one. Dinner at half past seven. The schedule was as fixed as the positions of the stars, and deviating from it was unthinkable.

But Alastair was not here. And no one else would know if she sat at the table until nine o'clock, drinking tea that had gone lukewarm and staring out at the rain.

So she did.

She sat and watched the grey morning light move across the windows, and she thought about nothing in particular. Or rather, she thought about everything, in a loose and unfocused way that felt almost dangerous. About her life. About her marriage. About the years stretching ahead of her, identical to the years behind, a long corridor with no doors and no windows and no end.

The footman appeared at half past eight to inquire if she required anything further. She dismissed him with a word and continued sitting.

It was nearly nine when she finally rose.

On the second day, she took a long walk through the grounds.

This was another rebellion, larger than the first. Alastair did not forbid her anything, but he had once mentioned, in passing, that excessive walking was unbecoming in a duchess. She had filed this away with all the other small regulations that governed her existence, do not laugh too loudly, do not eat with obvious appetite, do not have opinions that might require defending.

The grounds at Fenleigh were extensive and well-maintained. There were formal gardens near the house, geometric beds of roses and lavender bounded by precisely trimmed box hedges. Beyond these lay rolling lawns that gave way to a small wood, and beyond that, fields belonging to the tenant farmers.

Isobel walked through all of it, her boots growing muddy, her hem trailing in the wet grass. She passed gardeners who tipped their caps and looked surprised to see her. She crossed a stream on stepping stones that were slick with moss. She climbed a small hill that offered a view of the countryside, brown and green and grey under the lowering sky.

At the edge of the wood, she stopped and turned to look back at the house.

From here, it appeared very grand and very remote. A monument to generations of Vane ambition, all pale stone and symmetrical windows. She had lived within those walls for three years. She could navigate its corridors blindfolded, could name every servant, could predict with reasonable accuracy which floorboards would creak and which doors would stick in damp weather.

And yet it did not feel like home. It never had.

Home, Isobel thought, was supposed to be a feeling. A sense of belonging, of rightness. She had felt it once, briefly, as a child, in the small sitting room where her nurse had taught her to read. The fire crackling, the smell of lavender, the feeling of being held within something warm and safe.

She had not felt it since.

Standing on the hillside, looking at the great house that belonged to her husband and would never truly belong to her, she wondered if she ever would again.

That afternoon, she visited the tenant cottages.

It was something she did periodically, bringing baskets of food and medicine to the families who worked the Fenleigh lands. The tenants expected it. The role of Lady Bountiful was one she had learned to play well, and she performed it with the same smooth competence she brought to all her duties.

But today felt different. Today she found herself looking at the people she visited, not as recipients of charity, but as individuals. People with lives and concerns and inner worlds of their own.

Mrs. Hobson, the blacksmith's wife, had a new baby. A girl, red-faced and squalling, nestled in a basket near the fire. Mrs. Hobson looked tired but happy, her face lit with a particular glow that Isobel recognized without being able to name.

"She's beautiful," Isobel said, looking down at the infant. "What have you named her?"

"Sarah, Your Grace. After my mother."

"A lovely name."

Mrs. Hobson beamed. "She's a good girl. Sleeps through the night already, mostly. Her father's besotted with her, of course. Won't put her down when he's home."

Isobel tried to imagine Alastair besotted with a child. The image would not form. She could not picture him holding an infant at all, let alone refusing to set one down.

"You are fortunate," she said.

"That I am, Your Grace. That I am."

She left the cottage with a strange ache in her chest. Not envy, exactly. Something more complicated. A recognition, perhaps, of all the things her life did not contain. Warmth. Joy. Connection.

She walked back to the great house with her empty basket, and the ache did not fade.

On the third day, a letter arrived from Charlotte.

Isobel carried it to the library, settled into her chair, and broke the seal with more eagerness than she allowed herself to show. Charlotte's letters were the brightest spot in her correspondence, full of gossip and complaint and the kind of irreverent observations that would have sent their mother into palpitations.

Dearest Izzy, the letter began. Charlotte was the only person in the world who called her that.

I hope this finds you well and not yet dead of boredom in that great mausoleum you call home. I confess I cannot imagine how you bear it. All that silence and propriety! I should run mad within a week.

But enough about your dreary existence. Let me tell you about mine. Mother has decided that I am to marry Mr. Edmund Fairfax, who is forty years old if he is a day and has the conversational abilities of a boiled turnip. He is, however, in possession of a decent fortune and no inconvenient first wife, which Mother considers quite sufficient recommendation. I am to meet him at the Harringtons' ball next week, where I am expected to be charming and demure and not at all the disappointment I usually am.

I have already decided to be exactly the disappointment I usually am. If Mr. Fairfax cannot appreciate my sparkling wit, he does not deserve my hand.

Do you think I am being foolish, Izzy? Sometimes I wonder. You married as Mother wished, and look at you, a duchess, no less, with a fine house and a handsome husband and everything a woman is supposed to want. Perhaps I should be more tractable. Perhaps if I simply surrendered, as you did, I might find contentment.

But then I think, no. I cannot. I will not become a ghost, drifting through rooms where no one sees me. I want to be seen, Izzy. I want to be known. Even if it means spinsterhood and penury and Mother's eternal disappointment.

Write back soon and tell me I am not mad. Or tell me I am, if you prefer. I only want to hear from you.

Your loving sister, Charlotte

P.S. I have enclosed a sketch of Mr. Fairfax that I made from memory after seeing him at church. I think you will agree that the turnip comparison is generous.

Isobel unfolded the sketch, which depicted a rotund man with a receding hairline and an expression of profound vacancy. Despite herself, she laughed.

Then she read the letter again, and the laughter faded.

I will not become a ghost, drifting through rooms where no one sees me.

Charlotte did not know, could not know, how precisely those words struck. She had written them carelessly, as she wrote everything, with no sense of how they might land. She did not know what her sister's life had become. How could she? Isobel had never told her.

She had never told anyone.

In her letters home, she wrote of the house and the grounds and the excellent quality of the local honey. She wrote of her charitable work and her pleasant relationships with the neighboring families. She wrote, occasionally, of Alastair, that he was well, that he was busy, that he sent his regards. She did not write about the silence at dinner, or the way he looked through her rather than at her, or the slow, creeping certainty that she had ceased to exist as anything other than a household function.

A duchess. A hostess. A manager of household affairs.

Not a person. Not Isobel. Not anyone at all.

She went to her writing desk and took out a fresh sheet of paper. She would write back to Charlotte, of course. She always wrote back. But this time, she paused before beginning.

What would happen, she wondered, if she told the truth?

Dearest Charlotte, she might write. *You ask if you are being foolish, and I tell you, no. You are being wise. Wiser than I was. I surrendered, as you say, and look what it has brought me. A fine house where I am lonely. A handsome husband who does not see me. Everything a woman is supposed to want, and none of what a woman actually needs.*

Do not marry Mr. Fairfax. Do not marry anyone unless he looks at you as if you are the most interesting thing in the room. Do not settle. Do not make my mistake.

But she did not write any of that.

Instead, she wrote what she always wrote, pleasant news, mild encouragements, gentle humor that revealed nothing. She told Charlotte that Mr. Fairfax sounded dreadful and that she was right to be skeptical. She told her to trust her instincts and to write again soon.

She did not tell her the truth.

She was not certain, anymore, that she knew how.

On the fourth day, she found herself standing in front of the looking glass in her bedchamber.

It was not something she did often. She dressed each morning with Mary's help, consulting the mirror only to ensure that her hair was in place and her gown was properly fastened. She did not linger. She did not study her reflection. She did not ask herself the questions that mirrors seemed to invite.

But today, for reasons she could not quite name, she looked.

The woman in the glass was familiar in the way that furniture is familiar, or the view from a window one passes every day. Pleasant features, neither beautiful nor plain. Brown hair that curled slightly at the temples when the weather was damp. Grey eyes, set wide apart, with a hint of something, intelligence perhaps, or sadness, lurking in their depths.

She was thirty years old. Not young anymore, but not old. The years had been kind to her face, or perhaps simply indifferent. She looked, she thought, exactly like what she was, a well-bred woman of the English gentry, unremarkable in every way.

No one would look at her and see anything unusual. No one would suspect the hollowness inside her, the slow erosion of self that had been happening for years. She had learned to hide it so well that even she sometimes forgot it was there.

Until moments like this, when she looked in the mirror and saw a stranger.

Who are you? she asked silently. *What do you want? What are you here for?*

The woman in the glass had no answers. She simply stared back, patient and empty, waiting for instructions.

That night, she wrote in her journal,

Charlotte asked if I had found contentment in my marriage. I did not answer her directly. I could not. How does one explain that contentment is not the same as happiness? That one can be content in the way a well-fed animal is content, warm, sheltered, undisturbed, without ever once feeling joy?

I do not think Alastair is unhappy with me. I do not think he thinks of me enough to be unhappy. I am a piece of the household machinery, functioning as expected. One does not feel emotion toward a well-oiled hinge.

But Charlotte's letter has unsettled me. She speaks of wanting to be seen, to be known. She speaks as if this is a reasonable thing to want, as if it is not greedy or improper to wish for more than shelter and provision.

I was taught that such wishes were dangerous. That a woman who wanted too much would always be disappointed. That gratitude was the highest virtue and dissatisfaction the greatest sin.

I have been grateful. I have been so careful to be grateful.

And yet.

She stopped writing. The candle had burned low, and shadows were pooling in the corners of the room. Beyond the window, the moon was rising, thin and pale.

And yet, she had written. But she did not know how to finish the thought.

There was something stirring in her, something small and tentative, like a seed beginning to split its shell. She did not have a name for it yet. She was not certain she wanted one.

She only knew that Charlotte's words had lodged somewhere inside her, and she could not seem to shake them loose.

I will not become a ghost.

But what if one already had?

What then?

Chapter Three

Alastair returned from London on a Thursday, one day earlier than expected.

Isobel learned of his arrival not from him but from Mrs. Harding, who appeared at the library door with the particular expression she wore when the household was about to require more effort than usual.

"His Grace's carriage has been spotted on the main road, Your Grace. He should arrive within the hour."

"Thank you, Mrs. Harding. Please ensure his rooms are ready and inform Cook that we will dine at the usual time."

"Very good, Your Grace."

The housekeeper withdrew, and Isobel sat for a moment with the book open in her lap. She had been reading poetry, a small rebellion, since Alastair considered poetry an indulgence unsuited to serious minds. Now she marked her place and set the volume aside, her hands moving with the automatic precision of long practice.

She should go upstairs and change. She was wearing a simple morning dress, perfectly acceptable for a day alone but perhaps not quite formal enough to greet a returning husband. There were expectations to be met. Standards to be maintained.

She rose from the chair. Her body knew what to do; it had been trained to know. But somewhere behind her breastbone, a small resistance flickered. A reluctance that had no name and no obvious cause.

She paused at the library door, looking back at the chair where she had been sitting, at the book of poetry she had set aside. For two weeks, she had lived in this house on her own terms. She had lingered at breakfast and walked the grounds and read whatever she pleased. She had been, in some small way, free.

Now Alastair was returning. And with him, all the constraints that his presence implied.

The resistance flickered again, stronger this time. She pushed it down and went upstairs to change.

By the time Alastair's carriage rolled up the drive, Isobel was waiting in the entrance hall.

She had chosen a dress of deep green silk, one that she knew suited her coloring, though she could not have said why it mattered. Her hair had been repinned by Mary, and she wore the small pearl earrings that had belonged to Alastair's grandmother. She was properly attired, properly composed, properly ready to welcome him home.

The door opened. Alastair entered, brushing rain from his coat. He looked tired, she noticed. There were lines around his eyes that she did not remember seeing before, and something in his posture suggested weariness beyond the physical.

"Welcome home," she said. "I hope your journey was not too arduous."

"It was tolerable." He handed his coat to the footman without looking at him. "The roads are in poor condition. There was a delay in Grantham."

"I am sorry to hear it."

They stood facing each other in the entrance hall, the space between them filled with something that was not quite tension and not quite ease. Isobel searched his face for some sign that he was pleased to see her, that he had missed her, that her presence mattered to him in any way.

She found nothing. He looked at her as he always did, with the polite, distant attention one might give to a well-functioning piece of household equipment.

"I shall be in my study," he said. "There are matters that require my attention before dinner."

"Of course. Shall I have tea sent up?"

"Please."

He inclined his head and moved past her, his footsteps retreating down the corridor toward the east wing. Isobel stood alone in the entrance hall, the green silk dress suddenly feeling too formal, too careful, too much like costume.

The footman was watching her with carefully concealed curiosity. She straightened her spine and gave the order for tea to be prepared.

That evening, they dined together for the first time in two weeks.

The great dining room felt different now that Alastair was home. Smaller, somehow, despite its actual size. As if his presence compressed the space, drew the walls inward, made everything feel more contained.

Isobel sat in her usual place, precisely twenty feet from her husband. The candles flickered. The footmen moved silently around the table, serving courses with practiced efficiency. Everything was exactly as it had been before he left, and yet nothing felt the same.

"The business in London went well?" she asked, when the soup had been cleared.

"Well enough." He did not elaborate. He rarely elaborated. His life in London was a closed book to her, full of meetings and negotiations and concerns that he never shared.

"I am glad."

Silence fell between them. The sound of cutlery on china. The distant ticking of the clock. The soft footsteps of servants in the corridor outside.

Isobel had grown accustomed to these silences. In the early months of their marriage, she had tried to fill them, asking questions about his day, his work, his interests. But his answers had always been brief, almost grudging, as if conversation were an imposition on his time. Eventually, she had stopped trying.

Now she sat across from him and watched him eat, and she wondered, not for the first time, what he was thinking. Whether he ever looked at her and wished for more. Whether he ever felt the vast emptiness between them and wanted to bridge it.

She suspected she knew the answer. But she asked anyway, in her own mind, because asking was the only thing left.

"Is something the matter?"

Isobel looked up. Alastair was watching her, his fork suspended halfway to his mouth, his expression mildly curious.

"I beg your pardon?"

"You seem distracted this evening."

"Do I?" She reached for her water glass, using the motion to compose herself. "I apologize. I was merely thinking."

"Of what?"

The question startled her. He so rarely asked for her thoughts, her real thoughts, not the sanitized summary of household matters and social engagements. For a moment, she considered telling him. About the birds she had been reading about, the ones that migrated vast distances on instinct alone. About the creeping sense that she had somehow ended up in a life that did not fit. About the hollowness in her chest that seemed to grow larger with each passing day.

But even as she considered it, she saw his attention beginning to drift. His eyes moved from her face to the window, then to the clock on the mantel. Whatever momentary interest he had shown was already fading.

"Of the menu for next week," she said. "I had thought we might have the trout, if the fishmonger has any worth purchasing."

"That sounds acceptable."

He lifted his glass and drank, and the conversation was over.

Isobel looked down at her plate and felt something harden inside her. A small calcification around the soft tissue of hope. She had offered him an opening, and he had let it close. As he always did. As he always would.

She finished her meal in silence and excused herself as soon as propriety allowed.

Later, in her chambers, she sat at her dressing table while Mary brushed out her hair.

It was a nightly ritual, one hundred strokes, and Isobel usually found it soothing. Tonight, however, she felt restless. Her skin too tight, her thoughts too loud.

"Mary," she said, "do you ever feel as though you are living someone else's life?"

The brush paused mid-stroke. "Your Grace?"

"Never mind. It was a foolish question."

"Not foolish, Your Grace." Mary resumed brushing, her movements gentle. "I think perhaps we all feel that way sometimes. As if we've wandered into a play without knowing our lines."

"Yes." Isobel watched her own reflection in the mirror. "Yes, that is exactly it."

Mary was perhaps five years older than Isobel, a practical woman with kind eyes and a manner that was familiar without being presumptuous. She had come with Isobel from her father's house, the only piece of her old life she had been permitted to keep, and she knew more of Isobel's private thoughts than anyone else in the world.

Which was to say, she knew very little. But more than most.

"Might I speak plainly, Your Grace?"

Isobel met her eyes in the mirror. "Of course."

"You've seemed different these past weeks. Since before His Grace went to London. Not unhappy, exactly. Just..." Mary hesitated, searching for the word. "Awake. More awake than usual."

"Is that how it appears?"

"To me, yes." The maid finished the last stroke and began to braid Isobel's hair for sleeping. "I don't mean to pry, Your Grace. Only, if there is something troubling you, I hope you know that I would never speak of it to anyone. Whatever you might wish to say."

Isobel was quiet for a long moment. The fire crackled in the grate. Outside, the wind had picked up, rattling the windowpanes with irregular gusts.

"I think," she said slowly, "that I have been asleep for a very long time. And I am only now beginning to realize it."

Mary's hands stilled on the braid. "That must be a frightening thing, Your Grace. To wake up and find yourself somewhere you don't recognize."

"Yes." Isobel's voice was barely above a whisper. "Yes, it is."

"But perhaps," Mary said carefully, "it is also the beginning of something. The beginning of finding out where you actually belong."

It was the most presumptuous thing Mary had ever said to her. It was also, Isobel thought, the kindest.

"Thank you, Mary. That will be all for tonight."

"Yes, Your Grace. Good night."

The maid withdrew, and Isobel sat alone before the mirror. Her reflection looked back at her, familiar features, familiar eyes, nothing that would mark her as extraordinary in any way. She was handsome rather than beautiful, pleasant rather than striking. The sort of face that did not demand attention.

The sort of face that could disappear without anyone noticing.

She went to her writing desk and unlocked the journal.

The pen moved across the page almost without her volition, words spilling out like water from a cracked vessel.

He asked me what I was thinking. He actually asked. And for one moment, one single, fleeting moment, I thought, perhaps I have misjudged him. Perhaps there is more beneath the surface than I have seen. Perhaps if I only spoke, he would listen.

But then the moment passed, and I saw what I always see, his attention already sliding away, his mind on other matters. I could have told him everything, every thought I have ever hidden, every feeling I have ever suppressed, and it would have made no difference. He was not asking because he wanted to know. He was asking because it is what one asks. A social nicety. No different from "how do you do" or "I trust you are well."

I am not well.

I have not been well for a very long time.

And tonight, for the first time, I have admitted it. Not only to this page, but to myself.

She stared at the words. They seemed to pulse on the page, alive with a truth she had never before allowed herself to speak.

I am not well.

There it was. Simple. Undeniable. A diagnosis of the soul, rendered in black ink on cream paper.

She did not know what came next. She did not know how to fix what was broken, or even if it could be fixed. But the admission itself felt like something. The first crack in a wall she had not even known she was building.

She continued writing.

Mary said something tonight that I cannot stop thinking about. She said that perhaps waking up was the beginning of finding out where I actually belong.

Where do I belong? Not here, surely. Not in this house that has never felt like home, with this husband who has never seen me. But if not here, then where?

I do not know. I cannot even imagine.

But I am beginning, for the first time, to want to find out.

She closed the journal and sat for a long moment, her hands resting on its leather cover. The candle had burned down to a stub, and the room was growing dark.

Outside, the wind howled around the corners of the great house. But inside, in the quiet of her chamber, something new was stirring.

Something that felt, against all odds, like hope.

Chapter Four

The days that followed Alastair's return settled into their familiar patterns, but Isobel moved through them differently now.

She performed the same tasks, spoke the same words, maintained the same pleasant composure she had always worn like a mask. But beneath the surface, something had shifted. A lens had been adjusted, and everything she looked at appeared in sharper focus.

She began to notice things she had trained herself to overlook.

The way Alastair's gaze slid past her at meals, never quite landing on her face. The way he spoke to her in the same tone he used for the servants, courteous, impersonal, efficient. The way their paths through the house rarely crossed, as if they were planets in separate orbits, bound by gravity but never touching.

She had always known these things, in some distant, unexamined way. But she had filed them away as simply the nature of marriage, the inevitable settling of two lives into parallel routines. Now she saw them for what they were, evidence of an absence so complete it had become invisible.

He did not know her. He had never tried to know her.

And she, she had never demanded to be known.

At breakfast one morning, a week after Alastair's return, Isobel conducted an experiment.

She did not speak.

She took her usual seat, poured her usual tea, ate her usual toast with her usual deliberate care. But she did not offer the customary greeting. She did not ask about his plans for the day or report on household matters. She simply sat in silence, watching him through lowered lashes, waiting to see how long it would take him to notice.

He did not notice.

He read his correspondence, made his notations, drank his cooling tea. When he finished, he rose and inclined his head in her general direction, as he always did, and left the room. He had not looked at her once.

Isobel remained at the table, her heart beating strangely fast.

She had been silent for the entire meal. An hour of sitting across from her husband without speaking a word. And he had not noticed anything unusual.

She did not know whether to laugh or cry. In the end, she did neither. She simply sat there, in the pale morning light, and felt the last illusion of her marriage crack and crumble away.

That afternoon, she paid a call on Mrs. Whitmore, the vicar's wife.

It was not a visit she particularly anticipated. Mrs. Whitmore was a pleasant enough woman, but her conversation tended toward the predictable, parish gossip, her children's accomplishments, gentle complaints about the difficulty of finding good help.

Isobel had made these visits dozens of times and could navigate them without fully engaging her mind.

Today, however, something caught her attention.

They were taking tea in Mrs. Whitmore's small parlor, surrounded by the comfortable clutter of a home well-lived-in, when the conversation turned to a former resident of the village. A widow named Mrs. Bakewell who had, some years ago, removed to Cornwall.

"She has a little shop there now, you know," Mrs. Whitmore said, her tone carrying the particular note of scandalized fascination that marked truly interesting gossip. "A ribbon shop, of all things. Can you imagine? A woman of her standing, actually working?"

"I had not heard," Isobel said carefully. "Did she not have family she might have relied upon?"

"Oh, I am sure she did. But Mrs. Bakewell was always somewhat unconventional." Mrs. Whitmore lowered her voice, though there was no one else present to overhear. "Her marriage was not happy, you understand. After Mr. Bakewell passed, she simply left. Took what money she had and established herself elsewhere. There was quite a scandal at the time."

"I can imagine."

"The strange thing is," Mrs. Whitmore continued, leaning forward with the air of someone sharing a particularly choice morsel, "I had a letter from my cousin who visited that part of Cornwall last summer. She says Mrs. Bakewell seems positively transformed. Cheerful, energetic, quite content with her circumstances. My cousin could hardly believe it was the same woman."

Isobel lifted her teacup, using the motion to conceal whatever expression might have crossed her face. "How remarkable."

"Is it not? Though I suppose there is no accounting for taste. I should find such a life quite beneath me. But Mrs. Bakewell was always peculiar."

"What part of Cornwall, did you say?"

Mrs. Whitmore looked surprised by the question. "Trewarne, I believe. A small fishing village on the southern coast. Quite remote, from what my cousin says. Nothing like civilized society at all."

"How interesting."

The conversation moved on to other topics, the state of the parish school, the upcoming Easter services, the question of whether the curate would ever find a suitable wife. Isobel responded appropriately, nodding and murmuring in all the right places. But her mind had snagged on the image Mrs. Whitmore had painted.

A woman escaping an unhappy marriage. Establishing herself independently. Finding contentment in work and solitude.

It should have seemed scandalous. It should have seemed sad. A fall from respectability, a capitulation to circumstance.

Instead, it seemed like something else entirely.

It seemed like freedom.

On the way home from Mrs. Whitmore's, Isobel instructed the coachman to take the long route.

It was a small indulgence, but she wanted time to think. The carriage rattled along the country lanes, past fields brown with autumn stubble and hedgerows bare of leaves. The sky was grey and low, threatening rain that never quite came.

She thought about Mrs. Bakewell.

She had never met the woman. Had only heard her name in passing, as one of those former residents of the parish who had moved away and were now only mentioned in gossip. But the story lodged in her mind like a burr, catching on every passing thought.

Her marriage was not happy.

She simply left.

She seems positively transformed.

Was such a thing possible? Could a woman simply walk away from an unhappy marriage and begin again? The law said otherwise. A wife belonged to her husband, and her property, her income, her very person were his to control. Leaving was not merely scandalous; it was practically impossible.

And yet Mrs. Bakewell had done it. Albeit her husband had died though.

She had taken what money she had and established herself elsewhere. She had opened a shop. She had built a new life.

And she was happy.

The word struck Isobel with unexpected force. Happy. Not content, not resigned, not merely surviving. Happy.

When had Isobel last felt happy? She searched her memory for the feeling and found only distant echoes. Childhood moments, mostly. Her nurse reading to her by firelight. Charlotte's laughter in the garden. The particular satisfaction of mastering a difficult piece on the pianoforte.

Nothing recent. Nothing from her marriage. Nothing from the life she was living now.

The carriage rounded a curve, and Fenleigh came into view. The great house on its hill, all pale stone and symmetrical windows. Beautiful, grand, imposing.

A prison, dressed up as a palace.

Isobel looked at it and felt something shift inside her chest. Not quite hope. Not quite decision. But something adjacent to both. A crack in the wall. A sliver of light.

That night, she could not sleep.

She lay in her bed, staring at the canopy above her, while her mind turned over and over like a restless animal seeking comfort. Mrs. Bakewell. Cornwall. A ribbon shop.

It was absurd. She was a duchess, for heaven's sake. She had responsibilities, obligations, a position in society that could not simply be abandoned. The very idea of leaving, of walking away from Fenleigh and Alastair and everything she had been raised to value, was unthinkable.

And yet.

And yet she could not stop thinking about it.

What would happen, she wondered, if she simply left? Not dramatically, not in a rush of anger or despair. Just quietly. Deliberately. The way Mrs. Bakewell had done.

She had money of her own. Not much, but enough. Her father had settled a small sum on her at her marriage, pin money, he had called it, barely enough to signify. But she had been frugal. She had saved. And there were her mother's pearls, which had come to her when her mother passed two years ago. They were not valuable enough to make a fortune, but they were valuable enough to make a start.

A start toward what?

She did not know. That was the terrifying thing. She had no skills, no training, no preparation for any life other than the one she was living. She could manage a household, write a graceful letter, make pleasant conversation at dinner. None of these abilities would serve her in a ribbon shop.

But Mrs. Bakewell had managed it. Mrs. Bakewell, who had been a lady just as Isobel was a lady, who had been bound by the same rules and expectations, had somehow found a way through.

The thought was like a door, cracking open in a wall she had believed solid.

Isobel rose from the bed and went to the window. The moon was high, casting silver light across the grounds. Fenleigh looked beautiful in this light, ethereal, almost magical. A house from a fairy story.

But fairy stories, she had learned, were rarely kind to the women who lived in them.

She stood at the window for a long time, watching the moonlight move across the lawn. She did not make any decisions. She did not form any plans. But something had taken root in her mind, a possibility, fragile and tentative, that had not existed before.

Perhaps there was another life. Perhaps there was a door.

Perhaps, if she was very brave, she might one day walk through it.

The next morning, she asked Mrs. Harding a question.

It was a casual inquiry, slipped into their regular consultation about household matters, and Isobel was careful to keep her voice light, her interest seemingly idle.

"Mrs. Harding, I seem to recall a widow named Bakewell who lived in the parish some years ago. Do you remember her?"

The housekeeper's expression flickered, surprise quickly masked by professional neutrality. "Mrs. Bakewell, Your Grace? Yes, I recall the name. She removed to Cornwall after her husband's death, as I understand it."

"Do you know anything more about her circumstances? I confess I am merely curious. Mrs. Whitmore mentioned her yesterday, and I found myself wondering."

Mrs. Harding hesitated, clearly uncertain whether this was a test of some kind. "I did not know the family well, Your Grace.

Mr. Bakewell was not a tenant of the estate. But there were some whispers, after Mrs. Bakewell left, that the marriage had not been happy. That she had reason to want a fresh start."

"I see." Isobel kept her voice neutral. "And she has done well, I understand? Established herself in some sort of trade?"

"I would not know, Your Grace. Such matters are beyond my knowledge." But there was something in the housekeeper's eyes, a glimmer of understanding, perhaps, that suggested she knew more than she was saying.

"Of course. It is of no consequence. Merely idle curiosity." Isobel changed the subject, and the consultation continued along its usual lines.

But after Mrs. Harding left, Isobel sat alone in the morning room and thought about what she had learned. Mrs. Bakewell's marriage had not been happy. Mrs. Bakewell had wanted a fresh start.

Mrs. Bakewell had found one.

And if she could do it, perhaps, perhaps, Isobel could too.

That night, she wrote in her journal,

I have learned something today that I cannot stop thinking about. A woman from this parish left her unhappy marriage and established herself independently in Cornwall. She runs a ribbon shop. She is happy.

I know I should not dwell on this. I know it is improper, perhaps even dangerous, to imagine such a thing for myself. But I cannot help it. The thought has lodged in my mind like a seed, and I can feel it beginning to grow.

What if there is another life? What if the walls I have built around myself are not as solid as I believed?

I do not know if I have the courage to find out. I do not know if I will ever have the courage.

But for the first time in years, I am asking the question. And perhaps that is enough. Perhaps that is the beginning.

She closed the journal and stared at the blank wall opposite her desk.

Cornwall. Trewarne. A ribbon shop.

The words echoed in her mind like a spell, like a promise, like a door waiting to be opened.

She did not know yet if she would open it. She did not know if she could.

But she was no longer certain that she couldn't.

And that, she thought, was something. That was a start.

Chapter Five

Lady Wellington arrived on the first Tuesday of the new month, in a carriage considerably more ostentatious than her nephew's and with twice the luggage.

Isobel received her in the main hall with all appropriate ceremony, flanked by the household staff and wearing her best afternoon dress. Lady Wellington was a formidable woman of sixty-three who had, by her own account, never suffered fools gladly and saw no reason to begin doing so now. She swept into Fenleigh like a ship entering harbor, her companion scurrying behind her and her sharp eyes taking in every detail of the house and its inhabitants.

"Isobel," she said, offering her cheek to be kissed. "You look tired. Are you sleeping well?"

"Quite well, thank you, Lady Wellington. I hope your journey was comfortable."

"It was tolerable. The roads in this part of the country are abysmal, as always. I trust my rooms have been properly aired?"

"Mrs. Harding has seen to everything personally."

"Hmph. We shall see."

Alastair appeared from his study to greet his aunt, and Isobel watched as his demeanor shifted almost imperceptibly. With Lady Wellington, he was slightly more animated, more engaged. He asked about her journey with what appeared to be genuine interest. He smiled, actually smiled, at one of her tart observations about the state of the inns along the route.

Isobel stood to the side, fulfilling her role as hostess, and felt something cold settle in her chest. It was not jealousy, exactly. It was more like confirmation of something she had long suspected but never quite articulated, Alastair was capable of warmth. He was capable of connection.

He simply did not extend these capacities to her.

The first week of Lady Wellington's visit passed in a flurry of activity.

There were dinners to be arranged, guests to be invited, outings to be planned. Isobel managed it all with her usual efficiency, ensuring that every detail was attended to while remaining largely invisible herself.

It was harder, somehow, with Lady Wellington in the house. The older woman missed nothing. Her sharp eyes followed Isobel's movements, noted her silences, catalogued her interactions with Alastair with an intensity that felt almost predatory.

"You manage the household well enough," Lady Wellington remarked one afternoon, when they were taking tea in the drawing room. Alastair had excused himself to attend to correspondence, leaving the two women alone.

"Thank you, Lady Wellington."

"Though I must say, you are quieter than I expected. When Alastair first wrote to tell me of his engagement, I imagined someone more spirited. Someone who might shake him out of his dreadful reserve."

Isobel's hands remained steady on her teacup. "I am afraid I have always been of a quiet disposition."

"Yes. So it seems." Lady Wellington studied her for a long moment. "Tell me, my dear. Are you happy here?"

The question caught Isobel off guard. She had expected observations about her management of the household, perhaps criticism of the dinner arrangements or the state of the guest chambers. She had not expected this.

"I am content," she said carefully.

"That is not what I asked."

"It is the answer I am able to give."

Lady Wellington's eyes narrowed. For a moment, something flickered across her face, recognition, perhaps, or understanding. Then it was gone, replaced by her usual expression of cool appraisal.

"I see," she said. "Well. Content is something, I suppose. Though I have always found it a poor substitute for happiness."

She did not pursue the topic further, but Isobel felt the weight of her observation for the rest of the afternoon.

On the third day of the visit, Lady Wellington raised the subject of children.

They were in the drawing room again, this time with Alastair present. The conversation had been meandering through various topics, the health of distant relatives, the prospects of the coming Season, the state of politics in London. And then, with the blunt directness that characterized all her communications, Lady Wellington turned to Isobel and said,

"Three years is rather a long time, is it not?"

Isobel did not need to ask what she meant. The question hung in the air between them, heavy with implication.

"These things are in God's hands," she said.

"God and other factors, I suspect." Lady Wellington's gaze moved briefly to Alastair, who had suddenly become very interested in the newspaper on his lap. "Have you consulted a physician?"

"I am quite well, Lady Wellington."

"Hmm. That was not my question."

Alastair cleared his throat. "Aunt, perhaps this is not the time..."

"On the contrary, I think it is exactly the time. This family requires an heir, Alastair. That is not a matter one can leave indefinitely to chance." She turned back to Isobel. "I know of an excellent man in London. Very discreet. Very effective. I shall give you his name before I leave."

"Thank you," Isobel said, her voice carefully neutral. "That is very kind."

But inside, something was tightening, hardening. The assumption that she was a vessel, waiting to be filled. That her primary value lay in her ability to produce children. That her own feelings about the matter were irrelevant.

She glanced at Alastair. He was studying the newspaper with intense concentration, his face expressionless. He had not looked at her once during the exchange.

Of course he hadn't.

That night, Isobel could not sleep.

She lay in the darkness, thinking about Lady Wellington's question, about Alastair's studied indifference, about the endless expectations that pressed upon her from all sides. Be a good hostess. Be a dutiful wife. Produce an heir.

Be anything, in other words, except herself.

She rose from the bed and went to the window. The moon was half-full, casting a pale light across the grounds. In the distance, she could see the edge of the wood where she had walked during Alastair's absence. It seemed very far away now, that week of small freedoms. Very long ago.

Lady Wellington would be here for another three weeks. Three weeks of scrutiny, of pointed questions, of being weighed and measured and found wanting. Three weeks of performing the role of duchess while something inside her slowly suffocated.

And then what? Lady Wellington would leave, and life would continue as it had before. The same silences at dinner. The same invisible walls. The same slow disappearance of everything that made her who she was.

Unless she chose differently.

The thought came to her unbidden, rising from some deep place she had not known existed. Unless she chose differently. Unless she stopped waiting for something to change and made the change herself.

Mrs. Bakewell had done it. A woman with fewer resources, less education, less social position. She had walked away from an unhappy life and built a new one.

Surely Isobel could do the same.

The idea was terrifying. It was impossible. It was also, she realized with a shock, the only thing that felt real.

The incident that crystallized everything happened three days later.

It was small, as such incidents often are. Nothing that would seem significant to an outside observer. Nothing that would merit mention in any account of their marriage.

Isobel was in the library, reading. She had found a volume of natural philosophy she had not yet explored, and she was absorbed in a chapter about the properties of light, how it could be bent and refracted, how a single beam could be separated into its component colors by passing through a prism.

Alastair entered without knocking. He was looking for a particular document, something to do with the tenant farms, and he began searching the shelves without acknowledging her presence.

She watched him move through the room, opening drawers, shifting books, muttering to himself about the disorder of the filing system. He was less than ten feet away from her. He never once looked in her direction.

She could have spoken. Could have offered to help. But she found herself frozen, held in place by a terrible curiosity. How long would it take him to notice her? How long could she sit there, in plain sight, before he realized he was not alone?

The answer, it turned out, was approximately eight minutes.

"It might be in the study," she said finally, when he had been searching in vain for some time. "I believe I saw some agricultural documents there last week."

He startled slightly, turning toward her voice with an expression of mild surprise. "Ah. Yes. Thank you."

He left without another word.

Isobel sat very still, the book open in her lap, the chapter on light forgotten. She felt as though she had been struck, though no blow had landed. It was not what he had done. There was nothing wrong with searching a library, nothing wrong with being preoccupied. It was what he had failed to do.

He had been in the same room with her for nearly ten minutes.

He had not seen her.

She was invisible.

That night, she did not write in her journal.

There were no words for what she was feeling. Or rather, there were too many, pressing against her ribs like trapped birds.

Instead, she lay in the darkness and made a decision.

It was not a dramatic moment. There was no thunderclap of revelation, no sudden surge of courage. It was simply a recognition, quiet and final, that she could not continue as she was.

She would leave.

Not tomorrow. Not next week. But soon. When the preparations were made, when the opportunity presented itself. She would take her small savings and her mother's pearls and she would go somewhere else, become someone else, build a life where she might, might, finally be seen.

She did not know yet where she would go. She did not know how she would survive. But she knew, with a certainty that surprised her, that she could not stay.

To stay was to disappear entirely. To dissolve into the wallpaper, to become indistinguishable from the furniture. To die by inches, while everyone around her remained blind to the death.

She had spent three years waiting to be seen.

She would not spend another.

In the darkness of her chamber, with the great house silent around her, Isobel allowed herself to feel something that had been dormant for so long she had almost forgotten its name.

Hope.

It was fragile, uncertain, easily extinguished. But it was there.

And she would tend it, nurture it, protect it with everything she had.

Until the day she was ready to act.

Chapter Six

The decision, once made, changed everything and nothing.

Outwardly, Isobel's life continued exactly as before. She rose at the same hour, dressed in the same manner, performed the same duties with the same quiet competence. She presided over meals, received callers, managed the household, and maintained the pleasant composure that had become her armor.

But beneath the surface, she was planning.

She could not leave immediately. That much was clear. A sudden departure would raise questions, invite pursuit, create scandal. If she was to go, truly go, with any hope of remaining gone, she would need to be careful. Patient. Strategic.

The first task was information.

She began with Mrs. Bakewell. A letter to Mrs. Whitmore, ostensibly seeking news of former parish members for charitable purposes, yielded the name of the town in Cornwall, Trewarne, a small fishing village on the southern coast, just as Mrs. Whitmore had said. A subsequent letter, carefully worded, went to an acquaintance in Truro who might have further details.

"I find myself curious about the region," Isobel wrote. "A friend has mentioned considering retirement there, and I thought perhaps you might share your impressions."

The lie came easily. Everything came easily now, she found, when there was purpose behind it.

The second task was resources.

Isobel took careful inventory of her possessions. Her pin money, accumulated over three years of careful saving, amounted to nearly forty pounds. It was a pitiful sum for a duchess, but she had never been extravagant. She had bought little for herself, ordered few new gowns, indulged in no expensive habits. The money had simply accumulated, sitting in a drawer in her writing desk, waiting for a purpose she had not known existed.

Her mother's pearls might fetch thirty more, if sold to the right buyer. She had made discreet inquiries at the jeweler in Grantham during a visit the previous year, curious about their value but not then considering selling them. The jeweler had appraised them at thirty-five pounds, perhaps more to the right collector.

Her personal jewelry, the pieces that had been given to her before marriage, not the Fenleigh family pieces that belonged to the estate, might add another twenty. A small brooch of garnets from her grandmother. A pair of sapphire earrings that had been a gift from her father on her eighteenth birthday. Nothing remarkable, but enough to matter.

It was not much. It was not nearly enough for a woman of her station to live comfortably. But for a woman willing to live simply? To work, even?

It might be enough for a beginning.

Lady Wellington's visit stretched, as predicted, into a fourth week.

Isobel managed her duties with increasing automaticity, her mind elsewhere, always elsewhere. She nodded and smiled and poured tea while calculating distances and costs and possibilities.

She had obtained a map of the southwest of England from the library, dusty and old but still serviceable. She studied it at night, tracing the roads from Lincolnshire to Cornwall, counting the days the journey might take, imagining herself moving southward and westward toward the sea.

Trewarne was barely a speck on the map. A small coastal town, remote and unremarkable. The kind of place where a woman might disappear.

The response from her acquaintance in Truro arrived on a Wednesday.

Mrs. Bakewell, the letter confirmed, *does indeed reside in Trewarne. She operates a small establishment selling ribbons, lace, and sundry items of haberdashery. She is considered somewhat eccentric by local standards but generally well-regarded. I understand she lets rooms above the shop when they are not needed for her own use.*

Isobel read this last sentence three times.

Rooms above the shop. Available for letting.

It was not a guarantee. It was barely even a possibility. But it was something concrete. A destination, a person, a place where she might land if she found the courage to leap.

She burned the letter in the grate and watched the ashes curl and blacken. No evidence. No trail. If anyone was to find her correspondence and wonder, they would find nothing of interest.

She was learning to be careful.

The third task was the most difficult, finding the opportunity.

Lady Wellington departed at last, with the same ceremony that had attended her arrival. She embraced Alastair with genuine affection and offered Isobel her dry cheek to kiss.

"You have been an adequate hostess," she said, which from Lady Wellington was nearly extravagant praise. "Remember what I said. About the physician in London. And other matters."

"I shall remember. Thank you, Lady Wellington."

The older woman studied her for a moment, her sharp eyes searching. Whatever she saw, she did not comment on it. She simply nodded once, as if confirming something to herself, and climbed into her carriage.

Isobel stood on the steps until the carriage had disappeared, just as she had done when Alastair left for London. But this time, the feeling was different. This time, she was not simply enduring an absence.

She was counting the days until she could create one.

The opportunity came sooner than expected.

A week after Lady Wellington's departure, Alastair announced at dinner that he would be traveling to Edinburgh. Business matters, he said. A dispute with a shipping company that required his personal attention. He expected to be gone a month, possibly longer.

"So long?" Isobel said, keeping her voice neutral.

"The matter is complex. I cannot resolve it by correspondence." He cut a piece of beef, his attention already elsewhere. "You will manage the household in my absence, as always."

"Of course."

"Is there anything you require before I go?"

The familiar question. The question he always asked, as if ticking items off a list. She gave the familiar answer.

"Nothing, thank you. I hope the journey is not too arduous."

"I shall manage."

That was all. He returned to his meal, and Isobel returned to hers, and the silence settled around them like snow.

But inside, her heart was racing.

A month. Possibly longer.

It was more time than she had dared hope for. Time enough to make final preparations, to settle her affairs, to write the letters that would need to be written. Time enough to disappear so thoroughly that by the time he returned, she would be beyond easy finding.

She did not let herself feel the relief. Not yet. There was too much still to be done.

The next two weeks were a careful dance of preparation and concealment.

She wrote to Mrs. Bakewell, using a false name and posting the letter from the village when she went to visit the vicar's wife. She inquired, in the most general terms, about the possibility of lodging and the need for assistance in the shop.

I am a widow, she wrote, *seeking a quiet life by the sea. I have some experience with household management and bookkeeping, though I confess I have never worked in a shop. If you might consider taking on someone in need of a fresh start, I would be grateful for the opportunity to discuss terms.*

It was not entirely a lie. Widow was a kind of death, after all. And she was dying here, a little more each day.

The response came through the same circuitous route, Mrs. Bakewell had no immediate need of help but would be willing to consider an arrangement if the applicant proved suitable. The rooms above the shop were available for three shillings a week, meals included.

Three shillings. Less than Isobel spent on ribbons for her own gowns.

It was not a promise. But it was an open door.

She packed slowly, carefully, taking only what she could reasonably carry.

Two plain dresses, purchased with her own money during a trip to Grantham. She had told the shopkeeper she was buying them for a poor relation, and the woman had not questioned her. The dresses were simple cotton, serviceable rather than fashionable, the sort of thing a shopkeeper's assistant might wear.

Sturdy boots. A warm cloak. A few personal items that would not be missed, her journal, of course. A miniature of Charlotte that she had commissioned years ago. A small sewing kit. A book of poetry that she could not bear to leave behind.

She looked at the pile of belongings, so small it barely filled a single traveling case, and felt a strange mixture of grief and exhilaration.

This was her life. Everything that truly belonged to her, everything she could take with her into the unknown. It amounted to almost nothing.

And yet it felt like everything.

She sold her mother's pearls to a jeweler in Grantham, making the journey on a day when the household believed her to be visiting a sick tenant.

The jeweler was a small, neat man with spectacles and an air of professional discretion. He examined the pearls carefully, holding them up to the light, testing their weight.

"Thirty-two pounds," he said finally. "They are good quality, but the market for pearls is not what it was."

It was less than she had hoped, but more than she had feared. She accepted the money, tucked the banknotes into her reticule, and left the shop with her heart pounding.

She had sold her mother's pearls. She had taken an irrevocable step.

There was no going back now.

She arranged for transportation, a seat on the mail coach that stopped in the village twice weekly, continuing south through Lincoln and Leicester before eventually reaching the West Country.

The booking office was a small room at the back of the posting inn, staffed by a clerk who barely looked up from his ledger.

"Name?" he asked.

"Mrs. Smith."

"Destination?"

"Exeter." She had decided not to book all the way to Trewarne. Better to break the journey into stages, to leave a trail that went cold before it reached its true destination.

"That'll be two pounds, four shillings. Departure Tuesday at seven o'clock sharp."

She paid in cash, using coins she had saved for precisely this purpose. The clerk wrote her a receipt and handed it over without interest.

She was just another traveler. Another anonymous woman with a common name and a forgettable face.

It was, she thought, the most liberating thing she had ever experienced.

And through all of it, she continued to perform her role as the Duchess of Fenleigh.

She received callers and paid calls. She consulted with Mrs. Harding about matters domestic and with Cook about matters culinary.

She was, in every visible way, exactly the wife she had always been.

But inside, she was already gone.

The night before Alastair's departure for Edinburgh, Isobel lay awake in her bed and allowed herself to feel what she had been suppressing for weeks.

Fear. There was fear, certainly. Fear of the unknown, fear of failure, fear of what she was about to do. But beneath the fear, something else.

Possibility.

For three years, she had lived as if her life were fixed, immutable, written in stone. She had believed, been taught to believe, that a woman's course was set at marriage and could not be altered. That duty was the highest good and contentment the most a wife could hope for.

Now she knew differently.

She could choose. She could act. She could walk through a door into a life she built for herself, with her own hands, by her own decisions.

It might be terrible. It might be wonderful. It might be something in between. But it would be hers.

In the darkness, Isobel whispered the words aloud, testing them, "I am leaving."

They sounded strange. Impossible. True.

She closed her eyes and waited for morning.

Chapter Seven

Alastair departed for Edinburgh on a grey morning that promised rain.

Isobel stood on the front steps, as she always did, wearing her blue pelisse and her pleasant expression. She watched him climb into the carriage. She raised her hand in farewell. She said all the expected things, safe journey, good fortune with the business, she would write if anything required his attention.

He nodded. He thanked her. He settled into the carriage seat and opened a leather portfolio of documents before the horses had even begun to move.

The carriage rolled down the drive, turned at the gate, and disappeared behind the hedgerow.

Isobel remained on the steps until the sound of hooves had faded entirely. The drizzle had begun, soft and persistent, spotting her pelisse with dark points of damp. She did not mind. She barely noticed.

She was free.

No. Not yet. But soon.

She turned and went inside.

She had three days.

Three days to finalize her preparations, to tie up loose ends, to say goodbyes that could not be spoken aloud. It was not much time, but it would have to be enough.

The first day was for letters.

She sat at her writing desk in the morning room, the door closed against interruption, and wrote the most difficult correspondence of her life.

The first letter was to Charlotte.

Dearest Charlotte, she began,

By the time you receive this, I will have made a significant change in my circumstances. I cannot tell you the details, not yet, but I want you to know that I am safe and well and that the choice I have made is my own.

Please do not worry for me. Please do not try to find me. When the time is right, I will write to you again and tell you everything. For now, I ask only for your trust and your silence.

You once wrote to me about the fear of becoming a ghost, drifting through rooms where no one sees you. Those words lodged in my heart and would not leave. They helped me understand what I needed to do.

I am not a ghost anymore, Charlotte. Or if I am, I am a ghost who is choosing to walk through walls rather than remain trapped behind them.

I love you. I always have. And I hope that when you know the truth, you will understand why I had to go.

Your loving sister, Isobel

She sealed the letter and set it aside. She would post it the morning she left, timed so that it would not arrive until she was already beyond easy finding.

The second letter was to Mrs. Harding.

This one was simpler, a tissue of lies designed to buy her time. *Mrs. Harding,* she wrote,

I have received urgent word that my aunt in Bath has fallen gravely ill and requires my immediate attendance. I do not know how long I shall be away, but I trust you will manage the household admirably in my absence.

Please do not disturb His Grace with this matter. The journey to Edinburgh is long, and I would not wish him to cut it short on my account. I shall write to him myself when I have more information.

My maid Mary will remain here to see to my things. If you have any questions, please consult with her.

I am grateful for your many years of faithful service.

With appreciation, Isobel Vane, Duchess of Fenleigh

It was not a good lie. It would not hold up to scrutiny. But it did not need to hold for long. A few days, perhaps a week. By then, she would be in Cornwall, and the trail would be cold.

The third letter was the hardest.

She sat for an hour, staring at the blank page, searching for words that did not exist. How did one explain three years of accumulated loneliness to a man who had never noticed it? How did one articulate the particular grief of being provided for but not present to?

In the end, she wrote simply,

Dear Alastair,

By the time you read this, I shall be gone. I do not write to blame you or to cause scandal. I write only to explain, as best I can, why I could not continue.

You have not harmed me. You have never raised a hand or a voice against me. In all material respects, you have been a model husband.

But I have been invisible in this marriage, and I cannot bear it any longer.

I have tried to be what you needed. What my family needed. What everyone expected. But in becoming those things, I have ceased to be anything at all.

I do not blame you for this. I blame myself, for believing that invisibility was the price of security, and for paying it so long without protest. But I am done paying now.

I will not tell you where I am going. I ask that you do not search for me. Whatever scandal this causes, I will bear it. Whatever shame attaches to my name, I accept it. These are the costs of my freedom, and I pay them willingly.

I am sorry for any pain this causes you. I am sorry we could not be different than we were. But I am not sorry for leaving.

For the first time in three years, I am choosing my own course.

Isobel

She read the letter twice, folded it, and sealed it with plain wax. No crest. No mark. Just her words, waiting to be found.

She placed it on his desk in the study, weighted down with a paperweight so it would not be missed. Then she closed the door and walked away.

The second day was for goodbyes.

Not spoken goodbyes. Those were impossible. But silent ones, paid in glances and lingering looks, in the careful attention she gave to each corner of the house she would never see again.

She walked through the formal gardens, trailing her fingers over the box hedges she had helped to shape. She visited the library one last time, running her hands along the spines of books she had loved. She sat in her chair by the window and watched the light move across the room, memorizing the particular quality of the afternoon sun.

She found Mary in her chambers, laying out clothes for the next day.

"Mary," she said, "I want you to know that whatever happens, I am grateful for your service. You have been a good companion to me."

The maid looked up, her expression puzzled. "Is something wrong, Your Grace?"

"No. Nothing is wrong." Isobel managed a smile. "I simply felt I had not said it often enough."

"Thank you, Your Grace. It has been my honor."

She wanted to tell Mary the truth. To take her into her confidence, to have one person in the world who knew what she was doing and why. But she could not. Mary's loyalty was to the household, ultimately, and Isobel could not put her in the position of having to choose between her mistress and her conscience.

So she said nothing more. And Mary, though her expression remained puzzled, did not press.

That night, Isobel opened her journal for the last time.

She had decided not to take it with her. It was too dangerous, too revealing. If she was found and the journal discovered, it would tell her whole story, the loneliness, the despair, the careful plotting. Better to leave it behind, hidden where only the most thorough search would find it.

But first, she wanted to write one last entry.

Tomorrow I leave, she wrote.

I am terrified. I am exhilarated. I do not know what waits for me on the other side of this door, but I know that I can no longer stay on this side.

If anyone ever reads these words, if Alastair ever finds this journal and wonders what happened to the woman he married, I want him to understand, I did not leave because of something he did. I left because of something he did not do. He did not see me. He never tried.

I am not made of stone. I am not built to withstand endless indifference. I needed to be seen, to be known, to matter. And when I understood that I would never have these things here, I knew I had to go.

I do not know if I will find what I am looking for. I do not know if what I am looking for even exists. But I would rather search for it, even if I fail, even if I starve, even if I die alone in some unfamiliar place, than spend another day in this beautiful house where no one knows my name.

Goodbye, Fenleigh.

Goodbye, Alastair.

Goodbye to the woman I was supposed to be.

And hello, perhaps, to the woman I might yet become.

She closed the journal, locked it in the hidden compartment of her desk, and went to bed for the last time as the Duchess of Fenleigh.

On the third day, she left.

She rose before dawn, dressed in her plainest gown, and packed the last of her belongings into her traveling case. Mary had been given the day off, a small kindness, and a necessary precaution. Isobel could not have borne her maid's questions, and she would not have lied to her.

The house was quiet. The servants were still abed, or working in the kitchens preparing for a day that would proceed without her. She moved through the corridors like a ghost, which was, she thought, only fitting. She had been a ghost here for three years. Now she was simply making it official.

She left the letter for Mrs. Harding on the hall table, with instructions that it was not to be opened until the following day. She left her keys in the drawer where they belonged, and her household accounts neatly arranged, and every detail in perfect order.

A duchess to the last.

Then she picked up her traveling case, walked out the servants' entrance, and did not look back.

The village was two miles distant, and Isobel walked it in the pale grey light before sunrise.

The air was cool and damp, and her boots grew muddy within the first quarter-mile, but she barely noticed. Her heart was pounding in her chest, and her breath came fast, and every step felt like the first step of a new life.

She had imagined this walk so many times. Rehearsed it in her mind while lying awake at night, while sitting through silent dinners, while performing the endless small duties of her position. Now that it was real, it felt both familiar and utterly strange.

The village appeared ahead of her, its rooftops emerging from the mist. The church spire. The market square. The posting inn where the mail coach would arrive at seven o'clock.

She was going to do it. She was actually going to do it.

She felt a sob rising in her throat and forced it down. There would be time for tears later. Now there was only the next step, and the next, and the next.

The mail coach arrived at seven o'clock precisely as scheduled.

It was a large, lumbering vehicle, painted in the faded red and black of the postal service, with passengers already crowded onto the roof and inside the compartments. Isobel claimed her seat, paid for in advance, under a false name, and squeezed herself into a corner of the interior, her traveling case clutched on her lap.

The other passengers paid her no attention. She was just another traveler, unremarkable in her plain dress and serviceable bonnet. No one would look at her and see a duchess. No one would wonder who she was or where she was going.

She was invisible, still. But this time, the invisibility was a gift.

The coachman shouted. The horses strained against their harness. The wheels began to turn.

And Isobel watched through the window as the village receded behind her. The church spire. The market square. The familiar landmarks she had passed a hundred times on her way to pay calls and distribute charity baskets.

Then the road curved, and the village disappeared behind a line of trees.

She was gone.

The journey south took five days.

It was uncomfortable, exhausting, and frequently terrifying. The coach was crowded and poorly sprung, jolting over rutted roads that seemed designed to test the endurance of passengers and horses alike. At night, they stopped at coaching inns that ranged from tolerable to appalling, cramped rooms, thin mattresses, meals of questionable provenance.

Isobel bore it all in silence.

She spoke little to her fellow passengers, deflecting questions with vague replies about visiting family in the West Country. She ate when food was available and slept when sleep was possible. She watched the landscape change through the coach window, the flat fields of Lincolnshire giving way to the rolling hills of the Midlands, then to the wilder, greener country of the southwest.

With each mile that passed, she felt something loosening in her chest. The fear was still there, would never fully disappear, she suspected. But it was being slowly crowded out by something else.

Possibility. Space. Room to breathe.

On the evening of the fifth day, the coach crested a hill, and Isobel saw the sea.

It was her first glimpse of the ocean. She had never traveled to the coast, never seen anything larger than the ornamental lake at Fenleigh. Now, suddenly, there it was, grey and vast and endless, stretching to a horizon she could not see.

She pressed her face to the window and stared.

"Beautiful, isn't it?" said the woman beside her, a farmer's wife, traveling to visit her daughter.

"Yes," Isobel said. Her voice came out strange, thick with an emotion she could not name. "Yes, it is."

The coach descended toward the coast, and the sea disappeared behind the hills. But Isobel had seen it. She had seen it, and it had looked like freedom.

She arrived in Trewarne at midday on a Saturday.

It was a small town, smaller than she had imagined, clustered around a harbor where fishing boats bobbed gently in the tide. The streets were narrow and steep, paved with worn cobblestones, and the buildings were built of grey stone that seemed to have grown out of the cliffs themselves.

The coach stopped at a small inn near the harbor, and Isobel descended on unsteady legs. Five days of travel had taken their toll. She was exhausted, hungry, and more frightened than she had ever been in her life.

But she was here. She had made it.

She asked a passing boy for directions to Bakewell's Notions, and he pointed up the main street, toward a building with a faded sign and windows full of colorful ribbon.

Isobel picked up her traveling case and began to walk.

Mrs. Bakewell's shop was easy to find. It sat on the main street, between a bakery and a chandler's, with a wooden sign that read "Bakewell's Notions" in faded gold letters. The windows displayed bolts of ribbon in every color imaginable, along with lace, buttons, and various other small wares.

Isobel stood on the pavement for a long moment, her traveling case in her hand, her heart beating very fast.

This was it. The moment of truth. The leap into the unknown.

She could still turn back. Could still find a coach returning east, could still think of some explanation for her absence, some story that might be believed. The life she had left was still there, waiting for her, if she chose to return to it.

But she thought of the library at Fenleigh. Of sitting invisible while her husband searched for documents. Of three years of silence and distance and slow disappearance.

She thought of Mrs. Bakewell, who had escaped and survived and thrived.

She opened the door and stepped inside.

A bell jingled overhead. The shop was small and cluttered, crammed with more goods than its space could comfortably hold. Behind the counter stood a woman of perhaps fifty, with grey-streaked hair pinned back in a practical knot and sharp eyes that immediately fixed on Isobel's face.

"May I help you?" the woman asked.

Isobel set down her case. Her palms were damp; she clasped her hands together to hide the trembling.

"My name is Isobel," she said. It was the first time she had introduced herself without a title, without a family name, without any of the markers that defined her place in the world. "I wrote to you. About the room."

Mrs. Bakewell studied her for a long moment. Something shifted in her expression, recognition, perhaps, or understanding.

"So you did," she said. "I wondered if you'd actually come."

"I am here."

"So I see." Mrs. Bakewell came around the counter, wiping her hands on her apron. She was shorter than Isobel, solidly built, with the weathered face of someone who had spent time outdoors. "The room is upstairs. Small, but clean. Meals included if you want them. Three shillings a week."

"That is acceptable."

"Good." Mrs. Bakewell picked up Isobel's case as if it weighed nothing. "I'll show you up. You look like you could use a rest."

She led the way through a door at the back of the shop and up a narrow staircase. Isobel followed, her legs heavy with exhaustion, her mind strange and floating.

The room was small, as promised. Barely large enough for a bed, a washstand, and a single chair by the window. But the window faced the harbor, and through it Isobel could see the sea, grey and endless and free.

"It's not much," Mrs. Bakewell said, setting down the case. "But it's yours, for as long as you need it."

Isobel looked at the narrow bed, the plain walls, the small square of sky visible through the glass. It was nothing like the grand chambers at Fenleigh. It was nothing like anything she had ever known.

"It's perfect," she said. And meant it.

Chapter Eight

I sobel slept for fourteen hours.

When she woke, the light through the window had shifted to the amber of late afternoon, and for a long, disorienting moment, she did not know where she was. The ceiling was too low. The bed was too narrow. The sounds were wrong, no muffled footsteps of servants, no distant chiming of clocks, only the cry of gulls and the faint wash of waves against stone.

She lay still, letting the confusion settle, letting memory return piece by piece.

She was in Cornwall. She was in a rented room above a ribbon shop. She was, for the first time in her adult life, entirely alone.

The feeling that accompanied this recognition was complex, layered. There was fear, certainly. A cold thread of it running beneath everything else. But there was also something that might have been relief. And beneath that, something stranger still. Something that felt almost like peace.

She rose from the bed slowly, her body stiff from five days of travel. The room was cold; the fire in the small grate had burned down to embers. She wrapped her shawl around her shoulders and went to the window.

The harbor spread before her, painted in the warm light of approaching sunset. Fishing boats were coming in with the tide, their sails catching the last of the day's brightness. Men moved along the quay, hauling nets and calling to one another in accents she could barely understand. Children played on the shingle beach, their laughter carrying across the water.

It was so different from Fenleigh. So alive. So real.

She watched until the sun touched the horizon, until the sky blazed orange and pink and gold. Then she washed her face in the basin on the washstand, changed into her other plain dress, and went downstairs.

Mrs. Bakewell was alone in the shop, straightening a display of lace collars.

"There you are," she said, glancing up as Isobel appeared. "I was beginning to wonder if you'd died up there."

"I apologize. I did not mean to sleep so long."

"No need to apologize. You looked like you needed it." Mrs. Bakewell finished arranging the collars and stepped back to survey her work. "There's bread and cheese in the kitchen if you're hungry. Tea as well. Help yourself."

The kitchen was at the back of the ground floor, a small, practical space with a wood stove, a scrubbed table, and shelves lined with mismatched crockery. It was nothing like the vast kitchens at Fenleigh, where a small army of servants prepared elaborate meals according to rigid schedules. This was a room built for one person, or perhaps two, to feed themselves without ceremony.

Isobel found the bread and cheese where Mrs. Bakewell had indicated. She cut herself slices of both, poured a cup of tea from the pot warming on the stove, and stood at the table to eat.

She was ravenous. When had she last eaten with real appetite? She could not remember. At Fenleigh, meals had been performances, not nourishment. She had learned to eat like a bird, small precise bites, never appearing to want.

Now she tore into the bread like a laborer and felt no shame at all.

The cheese was sharp and salty, nothing like the delicate varieties served at Fenleigh. The bread was coarse, studded with seeds. The tea was strong enough to stand a spoon in.

It was the best meal she had ever had.

Over the next several days, Isobel learned the rhythms of her new life.

They were nothing like what she had known. Mrs. Bakewell rose early, before dawn, to prepare the shop for opening. There were goods to be unpacked, accounts to be tallied, displays to be arranged. The work was physical and constant, and Mrs. Bakewell did it all herself, with a brisk efficiency that left Isobel slightly breathless.

"You can help if you like," Mrs. Bakewell said on the second morning, when she caught Isobel hovering uncertainly by the door. "I won't turn down an extra pair of hands."

"I should like to help." Isobel hesitated. "Though I must warn you, I have never worked in a shop. I have no experience with this sort of thing."

"That much is obvious." Mrs. Bakewell's tone was dry but not unkind. "You hold yourself like a duchess and speak like you've swallowed a grammar book. But you're not stupid, and work can be learned. Start by sorting these ribbons by color. The customers like to see them arranged."

The task was simple, almost mindless, separating silks and satins into orderly piles of blue, green, red, gold. Isobel's fingers found their rhythm quickly, and as she worked, she felt something strange happening.

Her mind was quiet.

At Fenleigh, her thoughts had always been racing, planning, anticipating. Calculating seating arrangements and guest preferences. Tracking the movements of servants. Monitoring the mood of her husband. There had never been a moment when her mind was not working, churning, striving to stay one step ahead.

Here, sorting ribbons, there was nothing to calculate. Nothing to manage. Only color and texture and the simple satisfaction of order emerging from chaos.

It was, she realized, a kind of freedom.

By the third day, Isobel had established a routine.

She rose at dawn, when the first grey light began to creep through her window. She washed and dressed quickly, in the plain cotton dress that was already beginning to feel more natural than the silks she had left behind. She went downstairs to help Mrs. Bakewell prepare for the day.

The work was varied. There were shelves to be dusted, floors to be swept, stock to be organized. There were deliveries to be received and invoiced, accounts to be tallied and balanced. There were a hundred small tasks that, taken together, kept the shop running smoothly.

Isobel threw herself into all of it with an eagerness that surprised her.

"You take to this well," Mrs. Bakewell observed on the third afternoon, watching Isobel reorganize a display of buttons with methodical precision.

"I find I enjoy it." Isobel stepped back to assess her work.

"Because you're the one doing the doing."

"Yes. Exactly."

Mrs. Bakewell nodded slowly. "That's the thing about work. Real work, I mean. It gives you something that money can't buy."

"What is that?"

"The knowledge that you've earned your place in the world. That you're not just taking up space, but making something of it."

Isobel thought about this. At Fenleigh, she had always felt as though she was taking up space, filling a role that could have been filled by anyone. Here, sorting buttons and arranging ribbons, she felt like she was doing something that mattered, however small.

"I think I understand," she said.

"You will," Mrs. Bakewell replied. "Give it time. You will."

Later that day, Mrs. Bakewell asked her the question she had been dreading.

They were in the kitchen, sharing a simple supper of fish stew and bread. The shop had closed for the evening, and the town beyond the windows was settling into darkness. A candle flickered on the table between them, casting wavering shadows on the walls.

"So," Mrs. Bakewell said, breaking off a piece of bread. "Are you going to tell me who you're running from, or shall I guess?"

Isobel set down her spoon. Her appetite had vanished.

"I am not running," she began, but Mrs. Bakewell cut her off with a raised hand.

"You arrived in a mail coach with a single traveling case, wearing clothes that cost more than most people in this town earn in a year. You've never worked a day in your life, you jump at loud noises, and you flinch every time the shop bell rings, as if you're expecting someone to walk through the door and drag you away." She fixed Isobel with a level gaze. "Either you're running from someone, or you're running from something. Which is it?"

There was no point in lying. Mrs. Bakewell had seen through her from the moment she walked into the shop.

"My husband," Isobel said quietly. "I have left my husband."

"Ah." Mrs. Bakewell nodded as if this confirmed something she had suspected. "Was he cruel to you?"

"No. Not in the way you mean."

"Then what way?"

Isobel looked down at her bowl of stew, at the chunks of fish floating in golden broth. How to explain? How to put words to something as intangible as invisibility?

"He never saw me," she said finally. "In three years of marriage, he never once looked at me and saw a person. I was a function. A role. A piece of furniture that managed his household." She drew a breath. "I do not expect you to understand."

"Oh, I understand." Mrs. Bakewell's voice had softened. "I understand better than you might imagine."

Isobel looked up.

"My husband was the same," Mrs. Bakewell said. "Not violent, not drunk, not any of the things that would have given me reason to complain. Just absent. Present in body, absent in every way that mattered. I spent twenty years being managed and provided for and utterly invisible."

"What happened?"

"He died." Mrs. Bakewell shrugged, but there was something in her eyes that was not quite as casual as her tone. "Heart gave out one afternoon, sitting in his chair. The doctor said it was sudden, probably painless. I nodded and said all the right things and then went into the garden and laughed until I cried." She met Isobel's eyes. "Does that shock you?"

"No." Isobel's voice was barely audible. "No, it does not."

"Good. Because I'll tell you something else, and you can make of it what you will. The day I walked into this shop for the first time, the day I opened for business, sold my first ribbon, earned my first shilling by my own hand, that was the happiest day of my life. Happier than my wedding day. Happier than any day of my marriage."

"And you have never regretted it? Leaving your old life behind?"

"Not for a single moment." Mrs. Bakewell rose to clear the dishes. "Now. You can help me with the washing up, and tomorrow I'll start teaching you how to actually run a shop. If you're going to stay, you might as well be useful."

The next morning, Isobel's education began in earnest.

Mrs. Bakewell was a demanding teacher. She expected attention, precision, and a willingness to make mistakes and learn from them. She did not coddle or cushion. But she was also patient, in her way, and she took the time to explain not just what to do, but why.

"The customers are the heart of everything," she said, as they prepared the shop for opening. "Without them, we're just two women standing in a room full of ribbons. You have to learn to read them. What they want, what they need, what they're afraid to ask for."

"How do you learn that?"

"By watching. By listening. By paying attention to the small things." Mrs. Bakewell straightened a bolt of blue silk. "People tell you who they are, if you know how to look. Most don't bother looking. That's where we have the advantage."

Isobel thought of Alastair, who had never bothered looking. Who had never seen anything but the surface she presented to him.

"I know how to look," she said quietly. "I learned it in self-defense."

Mrs. Bakewell glanced at her sharply. "I imagine you did. Well. Put that skill to use here, and you'll do well."

The first customer of the day was a fisherman's wife named Mrs. Penrose.

She was a small, weathered woman with work-roughened hands and a harried expression. She wanted ribbon for her daughter's christening gown, she explained, but she wasn't sure what color, or how much, or what quality she could afford.

Isobel watched as Mrs. Bakewell guided her through the options. She noted how the older woman listened more than she spoke. How she asked questions that drew out what the customer truly wanted. How she made suggestions without condescension, offered alternatives without pressure.

By the end of the exchange, Mrs. Penrose had purchased three yards of cream silk ribbon and departed with a smile on her face.

"You see how that works?" Mrs. Bakewell said, when the door had closed behind her. "She came in not knowing what she wanted. She left feeling like she'd made exactly the right choice."

"You helped her decide."

"I helped her figure out what she already knew but couldn't articulate. That's half of what we do here. The other half is actually selling ribbons."

Isobel smiled. It felt strange on her face, unfamiliar. She had not smiled much, these past three years.

"I think I'm beginning to understand," she said.

"Good. Because the next customer is yours."

Isobel's first solo sale happened that afternoon.

A young woman came in seeking trim for a bonnet she was re-furbishing. She was shy, uncertain, clearly uncomfortable in the shop. Isobel remembered Mrs. Bakewell's advice, watch, listen, pay attention to the small things.

She noticed the woman's worn gloves, her carefully mended dress. She noticed the way her eyes lingered on the more expensive ribbons before moving, with something like resignation, to the cheaper options.

"Are you looking for something particular?" Isobel asked gently.

"Just some trim. Something simple. Nothing too dear."

Isobel selected several options and laid them out on the counter. She pointed out which ones would wear well, which would hold their color, which offered the best value for the price. She did not push. She did not pressure. She simply offered infor-mation and let the woman decide.

In the end, the customer chose a modest ribbon of forest green. She paid her coins with a small smile and departed, her purchase wrapped in brown paper.

"Well done," Mrs. Bakewell said from the back of the shop. "You have a gift for this."

"I simply listened to what she needed."

"That's the gift. Most people don't know how to listen." Mrs. Bakewell came forward and clapped her on the shoulder, a brief, awkward gesture of approval. "Keep it up. You might actually be useful after all."

That night, Isobel wrote in her new journal for the first time since arriving.

I have found someone who understands, she wrote. *Mrs. Bakewell knows. Not the details, I have not told her I am a duchess, and I do not think I shall, but the shape of it. The particular grief of being provided for but not present to. She lived it too. She survived it.*

And now she is teaching me to work.

The word feels strange in my hand. Work. I have managed, organized, supervised, but I have never worked. Not in the way Mrs. Bakewell means. Not in the way that produces calluses and tired muscles and a sense, at the end of the day, of having done something tangible.

Today I sorted ribbons for six hours. My back aches and my fingers are stained with dye. I have never been happier.

Is that absurd? Perhaps. A woman of my birth, finding joy in such humble labor? My mother would be horrified. Charlotte would laugh, but then she would understand. She always understood me better than I understood myself.

I should write to her. I should let her know I am well. But not yet. Not until I am certain this new life will hold.

For now, I am simply here. Sorting ribbons. Learning to work. Learning, perhaps, to be.

She closed the journal and sat for a moment, looking out at the harbor. The moon was rising over the water, casting a silver path across the waves.

Somewhere in Lincolnshire, Alastair would still be in Edinburgh, attending to his business matters, unaware that anything had changed. The letter she had left would remain unread for weeks yet.

But eventually, he would return. Eventually, he would know.

Isobel wondered what he would feel. Anger? Embarrassment? Relief?

She realized, with a small shock, that she did not particularly care.

Whatever he felt, it was his concern now. Not hers.

She went to bed and slept soundly, and for the first time in years, she did not dream of silence.

Chapter Nine

Three weeks into her new life, Isobel made her first sale entirely on her own.

It was a small thing, really. A length of blue ribbon for a fisherman's wife who wanted to trim her daughter's Sunday dress. The transaction took less than a minute, measuring the ribbon against the wooden ruler fixed to the counter, cutting it with the heavy shears that had already begun to feel familiar in her hand, wrapping it in brown paper, accepting the coins.

But when the customer left with her purchase and the bell jingled overhead, Isobel stood behind the counter and felt something shift inside her chest.

She had done that. She had served a customer. She had earned money. Not much, barely a few pence, but earned by her own hands, her own effort.

At Fenleigh, money had been something that simply existed, like air or water. It flowed through the household accounts, was managed by stewards and bankers, arrived and departed according to systems she understood but never participated in. She had never earned anything. She had only spent what she was given.

This was different. This was hers.

"Don't stand there gaping," Mrs. Bakewell said from the back of the shop, where she was unpacking a delivery of buttons. "There'll be others."

There were. Over the following days, Isobel served more customers, women from the town and the surrounding farms, coming for ribbon and lace and buttons and thread. She learned to measure by eye, to calculate prices in her head, to wrap parcels with the quick efficiency that Mrs. Bakewell had perfected over years of practice.

She learned, too, the art of conversation. Not the empty pleasantries of aristocratic society, but genuine exchange. She asked about children and husbands, about the fishing catch and the weather, about the small dramas that made up village life. The customers were curious about her, of course. A new face in a small town invited questions. But she had prepared a story, a widow from the Midlands, seeking a quieter life by the sea. It was close enough to truth to feel comfortable.

And if anyone noticed that her accent was too refined, her manners too polished, they were kind enough not to say so.

The work was hard in ways she had not anticipated.

By evening, her feet ached from standing on the worn wooden floors. Her hands, once soft and white, developed calluses from the shears and rough spots from handling coarse wool and linen. Her back complained from bending over the counter, and her eyes strained from sorting tiny buttons in uncertain light.

She loved every moment of it.

This was the revelation that surprised her most, the pleasure of tiredness earned. At Fenleigh, she had often been exhausted. From the mental strain of maintaining composure. From the emotional weight of invisibility. From the constant performance of a role that never quite fit. But it had been a hollow exhaustion, leaving her drained but unfulfilled.

Here, her tiredness came with satisfaction. She could look at the neat shelves, the organized displays, the account books balanced to the penny, and know that she had contributed to something real. Something tangible. Something that would not have existed without her effort.

"You're a quick learner," Mrs. Bakewell observed one evening, as they sat in the kitchen over cups of tea. The shop had closed for the day, and the lamp cast a warm pool of light across the scrubbed table.

"I have had good teaching."

"Flattery will get you an extra biscuit, but don't let it go to your head." Mrs. Bakewell pushed the tin toward her. "I wasn't sure you'd take to this, if I'm being honest. Gentry usually don't."

Isobel's hands tightened around her cup, but she kept her voice steady. "I am not gentry."

"No? You hold yourself like it. Speak like it too. The way you tilt your chin when you're thinking, the way you fold your hands in your lap." Mrs. Bakewell's eyes were sharp, assessing. "But I've noticed you never complain about the work. Most women of breeding would be horrified by what I've asked you to do."

"I am not most women."

"No." Mrs. Bakewell smiled, one of her rare, genuine smiles. "No, I don't suppose you are."

On market day, Isobel went into the town square for the first time.

Mrs. Bakewell sent her to purchase vegetables and fish for the week's meals. It was a simple errand, one she had supervised a hundred times at Fenleigh but never performed herself. Now she walked through the crowded stalls, basket over her arm, examining produce and haggling over prices like any ordinary housewife.

The experience was intoxicating.

At Fenleigh, she had never handled her own money. Purchases were made through servants, accounts settled by the steward, decisions about expenditure referred always to Alastair or the housekeeper. Here, the coins in her purse were her own. She counted them carefully, calculated what she could afford, made choices based on value and necessity rather than appearance or expectation.

She bought potatoes and carrots and a fine piece of cod. She bought a small pot of honey from a farmer's wife who threw in a sprig of lavender for free. She bought, after careful deliberation, a ribbon for her own hair, a simple thing of dark blue silk that cost only a few pence but felt like an extravagance.

She walked back to the shop with her basket heavy and her heart light, and she thought, *This. This is what it feels like to be alive.*

But there was still fear.

It came to her at night, mostly, when the shop was dark and the town was quiet and there was nothing to distract her from her thoughts. She would lie in her narrow bed and stare at the ceiling and think about what would happen when Alastair discovered her absence.

He would be angry. Or perhaps not angry, merely irritated at the inconvenience. He would send people to search for her, almost certainly. A duchess could not simply vanish without causing scandal. There would be questions, investigations, inquiries at coaching inns and posting houses.

How long before they traced her journey south? How long before someone remembered a woman matching her description, traveling alone, giving a false name?

Cornwall was far from Lincolnshire. Trewarne was a small town that attracted no attention. And "Mrs. Smith, a widow from the Midlands" bore no resemblance to the Duchess of Fenleigh.

She might be found. She had to accept that possibility. But she would not be found easily, and every day that passed made discovery less likely.

In the meantime, she had work to do. She had a life to build.

In her fourth week, a letter arrived from the Midlands.

Mrs. Bakewell handed it to her without comment, though her sharp eyes missed nothing. Isobel took it upstairs to read in private, her heart pounding.

It was from her aunt in Bath, the one who sent long, rambling letters about her health. Somehow, the letter had found its way to her through the forwarding arrangements she had established before leaving. Her aunt, of course, knew nothing of what had happened. She simply wrote as she always did, complaining of her rheumatism and the incompetence of her servants and the declining quality of the water at the Pump Room.

Isobel read the letter twice, then burned it in the grate.

It was a reminder that her old life still existed. That people still knew her, expected to hear from her, would eventually notice her absence. She would need to be more careful. She would need to sever those connections, gradually and naturally, so that her disappearance would seem less like flight and more like the simple drifting apart of distant relations.

It was a small thing. But it reminded her that she was not yet safe.

In her fifth week, a letter arrived from Charlotte.

It came through the post, addressed to "Mrs. Smith, care of Bakewell's Notions, Trewarne." The handwriting was familiar. Isobel recognized it before she even broke the seal.

She had written to Charlotte three weeks ago, using the same careful arrangements she had used for all her correspondence, a letter posted from a neighboring town, a false return address, no details that could be traced. She had told Charlotte only that she was safe and well and had made a significant change in her circumstances. She had asked her not to write back unless something urgent required it.

Charlotte had written back anyway.

Isobel carried the letter to her room and sat by the window to read it. Her hands were trembling.

Dearest Izzy, the letter began,

I received your extraordinary letter and have spent three weeks alternately celebrating your courage and worrying myself into fits over your safety. How like you to do something dramatic and then forbid me to respond! Did you really think I would obey? You know me better than that.

I will not ask where you are. I will not ask what you have done. If you do not wish to tell me, I shall respect your wishes, but only because I know you well enough to trust that you have your reasons.

What I will say is this, I am proud of you.

I do not know what brought you to this point. I do not know what finally broke through that terrible composure of yours and made you act. But whatever it was, I am glad of it. The sister I remember, the one who read forbidden books and had opinions she was never allowed to share, I had feared that sister was lost forever. Now I know she was only sleeping.

Be well, Izzy. Be happy. And when you are ready, when you feel safe enough to trust me with more, write to me. I will keep your secrets. I always have.

Your loving sister, Charlotte

P.S. Mother is furious, of course. She is telling everyone you have gone to nurse a sick relative in Scotland. I have not corrected her.

Isobel read the letter three times. Four times. Five.

Then she folded it carefully, pressed it to her heart, and wept.

The tears came without warning, without restraint.

She had not wept since leaving Fenleigh. Had not allowed herself the luxury of grief, had not had the time or the privacy or the safety. Now, alone in her small room with Charlotte's letter in her hands, she wept as she had not wept in years.

She wept for the marriage that had never been a marriage. For the years of silence and invisibility. For the woman she had been, slowly suffocating in a life that did not fit.

She wept, too, with relief. Charlotte knew. Charlotte approved. Charlotte was proud of her.

Someone in the world knew what she had done and did not condemn her for it.

It was such a small thing. Such a simple thing. And yet it meant everything.

When the tears finally subsided, Isobel sat for a long time in the fading light.

Charlotte's letter lay in her lap, creased now from being clutched too tightly. Outside the window, the harbor was settling into evening, the fishing boats returning, the gulls circling and crying in the purple sky.

She had been afraid, she realized, that she was alone. That her decision to leave had cut her off from everyone she had ever known, that she would spend the rest of her life in isolation, unseen and unknown.

But Charlotte had found her. Charlotte had reached across the distance and told her that she was not alone.

It did not solve everything. The fear was still there, the uncertainty, the knowledge that at any moment her new life might come crashing down. But it was easier to bear, somehow, knowing that somewhere in the world, there was someone who understood.

That night, she wrote in her journal,

Charlotte knows. Not everything, I have not told her where I am or what I am doing, but she knows I have left, and she is glad.

I did not realize how much I needed that. Someone to know. Someone to approve. Not of the scandal, perhaps, or the risk, but of the choice itself. Of the courage it took to make it.

She called me brave. I do not feel brave. I feel terrified most of the time, and exhausted, and uncertain of everything except this, that I would rather be frightened and free than comfortable and invisible.

Mrs. Bakewell says that courage is not the absence of fear but the decision that something else matters more. If that is true, then perhaps I am brave after all.

Perhaps I am becoming someone new.

Perhaps I am becoming myself.

She closed the journal and looked out at the harbor. The moon was full, and the water shone like silver.

In Lincolnshire, Alastair would be returning from Edinburgh soon. In a few days, perhaps a week, he would find her letter. He would know she was gone.

She wondered what he would do.

She wondered if he would understand.

And she realized, with a clarity that surprised her, that it no longer mattered.

Whatever happened next, whatever consequences came, she had made her choice. She was here, in this small room, in this small town, building a small life that was entirely her own.

For the first time in years, she was not waiting for someone else to decide her fate.

She was writing it herself.

Chapter Ten

By the end of her second month in Trewarne, Isobel had stopped flinching when the shop bell rang.

It was a small thing, but she marked it nonetheless. For weeks, every jingle had sent a spike of fear through her chest, the irrational conviction that this time, when she looked up, she would see someone she knew. A servant sent to retrieve her. A magistrate come to enforce her husband's rights. Alastair himself, cold and implacable, ready to return her to the life she had fled.

None of these things had happened. Day after day, the bell rang, and day after day, it heralded only ordinary customers, farmers' wives, fishermen's daughters, the occasional visitor from one of the larger towns up the coast.

She was safe. Safer than she had dared hope.

The realization settled into her bones gradually, like warmth returning to frozen limbs. She would never be entirely free of fear, she suspected. The possibility of discovery would always linger at the edges of her thoughts. But it no longer consumed her. It no longer defined her days.

She was learning to live again.

The shop had become familiar now, its rhythms written into her body.

She knew which floorboards creaked and which drawers stuck. She knew the best light for examining lace and the precise angle at which the afternoon sun hit the display of silk ribbons to show them to best advantage. She knew the customers by name, knew their preferences and their family situations, knew which ones would haggle and which would pay the asking price without question.

She had developed her own small improvements to the shop's operation. A new system for organizing the buttons, sorted by size and material rather than color alone. A ledger for tracking which items sold best in which seasons, so they could order more strategically. A display near the window that caught the eye of passersby and drew them inside.

Mrs. Bakewell approved of these changes, in her gruff way. "You've got a head for business," she said one afternoon, reviewing the latest figures. "Better than mine, if I'm honest."

"You taught me everything I know."

"I taught you the basics. The rest you figured out yourself." Mrs. Bakewell closed the ledger and fixed Isobel with one of her sharp, assessing looks. "I've been thinking about something."

"Oh?"

"I'm not getting younger. And this shop, it's more than one person can manage properly. I've been running myself ragged for years, too stubborn to admit I needed help."

"What are you saying?"

"I'm saying that if you wanted to stay, really stay, not just until you find something better, there might be a place for you here. A permanent place. Not as a lodger, but as a partner. Someone to share the work and eventually, when I'm too old to manage, to take over."

Isobel stood very still. The offer was enormous. Far beyond anything she had imagined when she first walked through the shop door with her single traveling case.

"You barely know me," she said carefully. "You do not even know my real name."

"I know you're honest. I know you work hard. I know you've been hurt by someone who should have cherished you, and I know you're trying to build something better." Mrs. Bakewell met her eyes. "That's enough to start. The rest can come later, if you decide to trust me with it."

The rest. Her title, her husband, the life she had left behind.

"I will think on it," Isobel said. "If you will give me time."

"Take all the time you need. The offer won't expire."

That evening, Isobel walked down to the harbor.

It had become her habit, this evening walk. When the shop closed and the work was done, she would make her way down the steep street to the waterfront, find a flat rock or a stretch of sea wall, and watch the sunset paint the water in shades of gold and rose.

She had never known how much she needed the sea until she found it. The vast, restless presence of it. The sound of waves against stone, constant and reassuring. The salt smell of the air, the cry of gulls, the sense of being at the edge of something infinite.

At Fenleigh, she had felt contained. Enclosed. The walls of the great house pressing in from all sides, the expectations of society hemming her in, the weight of her marriage crushing her into smaller and smaller shapes.

Here, at the water's edge, she felt she could breathe.

She found her usual rock and sat down, pulling her shawl tighter against the sea breeze. The sun was low now, touching the horizon, and the sky was streaked with color, pink and orange and deep, bruised purple.

A partner. A permanent place. A future in this small town, with this work that had come to feel like purpose.

Two months ago, such an offer would have been unimaginable. She had been a duchess then, with all the expectations and obligations that title entailed. The idea of running a ribbon shop, of spending her days measuring lace and counting buttons, would have seemed like a fantasy, or perhaps a nightmare.

Now it seemed like hope.

But there was still the question of Alastair.

She thought of him now, as the sun sank into the sea. He would have found her letter by now. He would know she was gone.

She had heard nothing. No letters, no messengers, no signs that anyone was searching for her. Perhaps he was not searching. Perhaps he had read her letter, shrugged his shoulders, and gone about his business. Perhaps her absence was merely another administrative matter to be dealt with, like a tenant dispute or a problem with the roof.

She did not know which possibility was worse, that he was searching for her, or that he was not.

If he was searching, she was in danger. Her freedom could be taken from her at any moment. The law was on his side; a wife belonged to her husband, and there was no legal mechanism by which she could simply walk away.

But if he was not searching, if he had simply accepted her departure without protest, then it confirmed what she had always suspected. She had never mattered to him at all. She had been so invisible that even her absence went unremarked.

Either way, she thought, the answer was the same. She could not accept Mrs. Bakewell's offer until she knew what her husband intended. Until she knew whether her new life could truly be permanent, or whether it was merely a pause before the inevitable reckoning.

The sun touched the horizon, flattening against the water.

Isobel watched it sink, the last light painting the clouds in shades of rose and amber. Around her, the harbor was settling into evening. Fishermen were securing their boats. Children were being called home for supper. The lanterns along the quay were being lit, one by one, small points of warmth against the gathering dusk.

This was her life now. This small town, this simple work, this room above the shop with its view of the sea. It was nothing like what she had been raised to expect. Nothing like what she had been trained to want.

And yet it was more than she had ever had.

Here, she was seen. Not as a duchess, but as Isobel. The customers knew her by name. Mrs. Bakewell valued her opinion. Even the fishermen on the quay nodded to her when she passed, recognizing her as a member of their community.

It was such a small thing. Such a simple thing. But it was everything she had been starving for.

Somewhere in Lincolnshire, Alastair was reading her words.

She imagined him finding the letter on his desk. Imagined his face as he broke the seal and began to read. Would there be surprise? Confusion? Anger?

She did not think there would be grief. You could not grieve the loss of something you had never noticed possessing.

But perhaps, perhaps, there would be something. A flicker of recognition. A moment of understanding. A realization, however belated, that the woman he had married was not merely furniture.

Or perhaps not. Perhaps he would simply file the letter away with his other correspondence and go about his business. Perhaps her departure would be nothing more than an inconvenience, a scandal to be managed, a problem to be solved.

She wondered if it would matter to him. She wondered if he would understand.

And she realized, sitting on this rock at the edge of the world, that she no longer needed him to understand. His comprehension was not necessary for her freedom. His approval was not required for her happiness.

She had spent three years waiting for him to see her. She would not spend another moment waiting for anything.

The next morning, Isobel wrote a letter.

Not to Alastair. That bridge was burned, and she did not wish to rebuild it. But to Charlotte, finally, with the full truth.

Dearest Charlotte, she wrote,

You asked, in your last letter, to know where I am and what I have done. I am ready now to tell you.

I am in Cornwall. In a small town called Trewarne, on the southern coast. I am living above a ribbon shop, run by a woman named Mrs. Bakewell who has become, against all expectation, a friend. I work in the shop each day, sorting ribbons and serving customers and learning what it means to earn my own way in the world.

It is nothing like the life I was raised to live. It is nothing like what Mother wanted for me, or what Father arranged, or what anyone expected when I married the Duke of Fenleigh. But it is mine. For the first time in my life, I have something that is truly mine.

I do not know what will happen next. I do not know if Alastair will search for me, or what I will do if he finds me. But I know this, I cannot go back. Not to that house, not to that silence, not to that slow disappearance of everything I am.

If I am found, if I am forced to return, I will not survive it. Not in any way that matters. The woman I was becoming in that house, the ghost I was turning into, she would have died by inches, invisible to the end.

I would rather live here, uncertain and afraid and utterly ordinary, than continue to exist like that.

Please do not tell Mother where I am. Please do not tell anyone. I trust you to keep my secrets, as you always have.

And if you ever find yourself in Cornwall, if you ever want to escape from Mother's matchmaking and Father's expectations and the whole grinding machinery of society, there is a room above a ribbon shop where you would always be welcome.

With all my love, Isobel

She sealed the letter, addressed it, and set it aside to be posted in the morning.

It felt like letting go. Like opening her hand and watching a bird fly free.

Charlotte would know everything now. And that meant Isobel was no longer entirely alone.

That afternoon, she gave Mrs. Bakewell her answer.

"I want to stay," she said. "I want the partnership you offered. I want to build something here, with you, for as long as circumstances allow."

Mrs. Bakewell's eyes narrowed. "For as long as circumstances allow. That's a careful way of putting it."

"My circumstances are complicated. There are things I have not told you, things I may not be able to tell you. But I can promise you this, as long as I am able to stay, I will give this shop everything I have."

"And if you're not able to stay? If these circumstances of yours catch up with you?"

"Then I will tell you the truth before I go. I will not simply disappear." Isobel met her eyes. "I owe you that much. You have given me a chance when I had nothing. I will not repay that with lies."

Mrs. Bakewell was quiet for a long moment. The afternoon light slanted through the windows, catching the dust motes that danced in the air. Outside, the sounds of the town filtered in, voices, footsteps, the distant cry of gulls.

"All right," she said finally. "I'll trust you. But know this, if your past comes knocking at this door, I expect you to stand beside me, not behind me. Whatever you're running from, we'll face it together."

"Together," Isobel repeated. The word felt strange in her mouth. She had never faced anything together with anyone.

But perhaps, she thought, it was time to learn.

That night, Isobel closed the shop.

It was a ritual now, this moment at day's end when she swept the floor and straightened the displays and prepared everything for the morning. She moved through the familiar space with something approaching contentment, her hands knowing where to reach, her feet knowing where to step.

The shop was quiet. Mrs. Bakewell had gone upstairs to rest, leaving Isobel to close up alone. It was a sign of trust, this small responsibility. A sign that she belonged.

She stood for a moment behind the counter, looking out at the empty shop. The ribbons gleamed in the fading light, silk and satin in every color of the rainbow. The buttons lay in their orderly rows, sorted by size and material. The lace hung from its hooks, delicate and beautiful.

She had helped to create this order. She had contributed to this small, functioning world. She was part of something.

It was not a grand life. It was not what she had been raised to expect. But it was hers, and that made all the difference.

Outside, the sun was setting over the harbor. Isobel went to the door, turned the sign from OPEN to CLOSED, and locked up for the night.

Tomorrow there would be more work. More customers, more ribbons, more small satisfactions and small challenges. The future was uncertain, and the past might still catch up with her.

But tonight, she was here. In this small town, in this small shop, building a small life that belonged to her alone.

Whatever came next, whatever consequences, whatever reckonings, she would face them as this new self she was becoming. Not a duchess. Not a wife. Not a function or a role.

Just Isobel.

For now, that was enough.

Chapter Eleven

The Duke of Fenleigh returned from Edinburgh on a Thursday afternoon, six weeks after his departure.

The journey had been productive. The dispute with the shipping company had been resolved to his satisfaction, the terms more favorable than he had initially anticipated. He had used the remaining time to attend to various other matters that benefited from his personal attention, meetings with bankers, consultations with solicitors, the careful maintenance of the commercial interests that sustained the Fenleigh estate.

He was tired. Six weeks of travel and negotiation had worn on him in ways he did not care to examine too closely. He was not a young man anymore, and the relentless pace of business took its toll. But he was satisfied with the work accomplished. That was what mattered.

The carriage rolled through the gates of Fenleigh and up the long drive. Through the window, Alastair watched the familiar landscape pass, the avenue of lime trees, the ornamental lake, the carefully maintained grounds that spoke of generations of

Vane stewardship. Everything was exactly as it should be. Orderly. Proper. Under control.

The house appeared as he approached, pale stone catching the weak autumn light. It looked, as it always did, like a monument. Something built to last, to endure, to stand as testament to the family that had created it.

He felt the usual flicker of pride at the sight. This was his inheritance. His responsibility. His legacy to preserve and, eventually, to pass on.

The carriage drew to a halt before the main entrance. Footmen appeared to attend to the luggage. The door opened, and Alastair descended, stretching legs that had grown stiff from hours of sitting.

Mrs. Harding was waiting at the door, her expression its usual careful neutrality. But there was something in her posture, some subtle tension, that caught his attention even before she spoke.

"Your Grace," she said. "Welcome home."

"Thank you, Mrs. Harding. I trust everything has been well in my absence?"

There was a pause. Almost imperceptible, but Alastair had learned to read the silences of his household. Something in Mrs. Harding's posture shifted, tightening almost invisibly.

"Perhaps Your Grace would like to refresh himself before discussing household matters," she said.

"Is there something that requires discussion?"

Another pause. "There is a letter waiting for you in the study, Your Grace. Her Grace left instructions that you should read it upon your return."

"Her Grace?" He looked toward the house, expecting what? Isobel to appear, as she usually did, pleasant and composed, ready to welcome him home? "Where is the Duchess?"

Mrs. Harding's face remained carefully blank. "The letter will explain, Your Grace."

Alastair did not go to his rooms to refresh himself.

He went directly to the study, ignoring the footmen who hovered uncertainly with his luggage, ignoring the dust of the road that still clung to his coat. Something was wrong. He could feel it in the air, in the strange quality of silence that seemed to hang over the house.

The study was exactly as he had left it. His desk, with its neat stacks of correspondence. His chair, positioned precisely. The familiar smell of leather and old paper and the faint lingering scent of the fire that had burned in the grate.

And on the desk, weighted down with a paperweight he recognized from his own collection, a letter.

He picked it up, noting the plain seal, the familiar handwriting. His name, and nothing more. No title, no honorific. Just, Alastair.

He broke the seal and read.

By the time you read this, I shall be gone.

The words did not, at first, make sense. Gone where? A visit to relatives? An unexpected journey? Some emergency that had required her immediate departure?

He read on, and the confusion gave way to something else. Something colder.

I have been invisible in this marriage, and I cannot bear it any longer.

He stopped. Read the sentence again. Read it a third time, as if repetition might change its meaning.

I have tried to be what you needed. What my family needed. What everyone expected. But in becoming those things, I have ceased to be anything at all.

Alastair sat down heavily in his chair. The letter trembled slightly in his hand.

I am a function, not a person. A role, not a wife.

He thought of Isobel. Tried to summon her face, her voice, the particular way she moved through rooms. But the images that came were strangely vague. Pleasant features. Brown hair. Grey eyes. She was always there, always present, always exactly where she was supposed to be. He had never needed to look closely.

Had never wanted to look closely.

I do not blame you for this.

But she did. Of course she did. The entire letter was blame, carefully wrapped in courtesy. Every sentence an accusation, every phrase a condemnation.

I ask that you do not search for me. Whatever scandal this causes, I will bear it.

She had left him. His wife, his duchess, had simply walked away.

Alastair set the letter down on his desk and stared at it. The room was very quiet. Through the window, he could see the grounds stretching away toward the wood, the same view he had looked at a thousand times.

Nothing had changed. And everything had changed.

He summoned Mrs. Harding.

The housekeeper appeared within minutes, her face still carefully composed, though Alastair thought he detected something beneath the surface. Apprehension, perhaps. Or pity.

"When did she leave?" he asked, without preamble.

"Six days after Your Grace's departure, as best I can determine. She left a letter for me as well, saying she had been called away to tend a sick relative." Mrs. Harding's voice wavered slightly. "I did not realize the true nature of her departure until I searched her rooms, Your Grace."

"You searched her rooms?"

"When two weeks had passed with no word, I became concerned. The letter she left for me said she would write with updates, but no correspondence came. I took the liberty of examining her chambers." Mrs. Harding hesitated. "Her personal effects are gone. Her jewelry, the pieces that belonged to her before the marriage, has been removed. Her writing desk has been cleared of all correspondence."

Alastair absorbed this. His wife had not left in haste. She had not fled in a moment of passion or distress. She had planned. Prepared. Executed her departure with the same quiet efficiency she had brought to managing his household.

The realization was somehow worse than the departure itself.

"No one saw her go?"

"The servants believe she departed early in the morning, before most of the household was awake. Her maid, Mary, had been given the day off. No one thought it unusual at the time."

"And there has been no communication since? No letters, no messages?"

"Nothing, Your Grace. I have made discreet inquiries among the staff and in the village, but no one has any information about where she might have gone."

Alastair dismissed Mrs. Harding with a wave of his hand. He needed to think. He needed to understand what had happened and why.

But his mind kept returning to the same phrase, circling it like a moth around a flame.

I have been invisible in this marriage.

He read the letter again.

Then again. And again, searching for some clue he might have missed, some explanation that would make sense of the inexplicable.

You have not harmed me. You have never raised a hand or a voice against me. In all material respects, you have been a model husband.

He had been a model husband. He was certain of that. He had provided for her, protected her, given her everything a woman of her station could reasonably expect. A fine house. A respected title. Pin money and fine clothes and the security of marriage to a wealthy man.

What more could she have wanted?

But I have been invisible in this marriage.

The word kept snagging in his mind. Invisible. What did that even mean? She had been present at every meal, every social occasion, every event that required a duchess's attendance. She had been visible to everyone. Acknowledged, respected, admired.

I am a function, not a person. A role, not a wife.

He thought of their dinners together. The long table, the careful conversation about household matters and social engagements. He thought of her pleasant composure, her quiet competence, the way she managed everything with such unobtrusive efficiency.

He had appreciated that efficiency. Had valued the smoothness with which the household ran under her management. Had been grateful that she required so little of his time and attention.

Was that what she meant by invisible?

He did not understand. He genuinely did not understand.

That night, Alastair did not sleep.

He sat in his study, reading and rereading the letter, as if different words might appear on the page. He paced the corridors of the house, noting the emptiness that had always been there but had somehow escaped his attention. He stood in the doorway of her chambers, stripped now of the small personal touches that had marked them as hers, and tried to remember what they had looked like when she was here.

He could not.

How was it possible to live with someone for three years and remember so little? He knew the color of her hair, the general shape of her face, the sound of her voice. But the details, the particular shade of her eyes, the way she smiled (did she smile? when was the last time he had seen her smile?), these had faded to vagueness.

She was right. He had not seen her.

The realization sat in his chest like a stone.

He returned to the study as dawn began to lighten the sky beyond the windows. He sat at his desk, the letter before him, and tried to think.

What should he do?

The practical answer was obvious. Send men to search for her. Hire investigators. Use his resources, his connections, his authority as her husband to track her down and bring her home. The law was on his side. A wife could not simply leave her husband. There would be scandal, certainly, but scandal could be managed. The important thing was to restore order. To return things to the way they had been.

But as he sat there, watching the light strengthen and the shadows retreat, another thought began to form.

What if she was right?

What if he had failed her in ways he could not even see?

I am a function, not a person.

He had never asked her what she thought. Never inquired about her interests, her opinions, her inner life. He had assumed that her silence meant contentment. That her efficiency meant satisfaction. That her composure meant she was well.

But what if her silence had meant something else entirely?

He began to search for clues.

Not for her location, not yet. But for understanding. For some evidence of who she had been beneath the pleasant surface he had never thought to look beneath.

Her chambers yielded little. The furniture remained, the drapes, the carpet. But everything personal had been removed. No letters, no keepsakes, no books that might reveal her interests. It was as if she had never lived there at all.

He questioned the servants, carefully, trying not to reveal the full extent of his ignorance. What had she done with her days? Whom had she spoken to? What had she enjoyed?

The answers were maddeningly vague. She had managed the household. She had paid calls on neighboring families. She had spent time in the library. She had been pleasant to everyone and close to no one.

"She was a very private person, Your Grace," Mrs. Harding said, when pressed. "She did not confide in the staff. She did not confide in anyone, as far as I could tell."

Not even her husband, Alastair thought. Least of all her husband.

On the third day, he went to the library.

It was, Mrs. Harding had said, where Isobel had spent much of her time. He had vaguely known this, had occasionally seen her there with a book in her lap, but he had never paid attention to what she was reading or why she was there.

The library was vast, filled with generations of accumulated books that no one in living memory had bothered to catalogue properly. He wandered through the stacks, running his fingers along the spines, trying to imagine which volumes she might have chosen.

In a corner near the window, he found a chair with a worn velvet cushion. It was positioned to catch the afternoon light, angled toward the view of the grounds. Someone had sat here often enough to leave an impression in the fabric.

This, he realized, was where she had read. This was her place.

He sat down in the chair, trying to see the room as she might have seen it. The tall windows, the endless rows of books, the dust motes dancing in the slanted light. It was beautiful, in its way. A sanctuary of quiet and solitude.

Had she been happy here? Or had this been another kind of hiding?

He did not know. He realized, with growing horror, that he did not know anything about her at all.

On the fourth day, he searched her writing desk.

Mrs. Harding had said it was cleared of correspondence, and so it was. The surface was bare, the drawers empty. But something made him look more closely. He ran his hands along the sides, checking for hidden compartments of the sort that fine furniture sometimes contained.

In the bottom drawer, he found one.

A small panel that shifted when pressed just so, revealing a space barely large enough to hold a slim volume. And in that space, tucked away as if it had never existed, was a leather-bound journal.

Plain brown calfskin. No gilding. No ornamentation.

Alastair's heart was pounding as he lifted it from its hiding place. He knew, without opening it, that this was what he had been searching for. Not a clue to her location, but something more important.

A window into her soul.

He carried the journal to his study, closed the door, and began to read.

Chapter Twelve

The journal began three months into their marriage.

Alastair settled into his chair, angling the candle for better light. The handwriting was familiar, the same careful script that had addressed his letters, managed his household accounts, composed the correspondence that kept his social obligations in order.

He expected, what? Complaints about the weather? Mild observations about household matters? Whatever ladies wrote about in their private hours?

The first entry disabused him of these expectations immediately.

Mother says I should be grateful. I have a husband of rank and fortune. A house that wants for nothing. A position in society that many would envy. She tells me this each time I write, as if I had forgotten, as if gratitude were something I required reminding of.

I am grateful. I remind myself of this each morning when I wake, and each night before I sleep. I list the things I have been given, counting them like beads on a rosary.

And yet.

There is a hollowness here that I cannot name. A space where something should be but is not. I look at my husband across the dinner table and I see a stranger. Not an unkind stranger, he has never been unkind, but a stranger nonetheless. A man I live with but do not know. Who does not know me.

Alastair frowned. Three months into their marriage, barely enough time to establish routines, let alone form deep connections. Surely she had not expected instant intimacy? Marriages took time. Everyone knew that.

He turned the page, expecting the tone to moderate as she adjusted to her new circumstances.

Six months today since my wedding. I marked it in my mind, though of course Alastair did not mention it. Why would he? It is not the sort of anniversary that signifies.

I tried, this morning, to begin a conversation with him at breakfast. I asked about his plans for the eastern tenants, a safe topic, I thought, one that would interest him. He answered briefly, without looking up from his correspondence. "The matter is in hand." That was all.

The matter is in hand. Four words, and then silence.

I wonder sometimes if he would notice if I simply stopped speaking altogether. If I became a piece of furniture, a particularly well-made chair, perhaps, or a decorative screen. Something useful, pleasant to look at, requiring no response.

Perhaps that is what I am already.

Alastair's jaw tightened. This was unfair. He had always answered her questions. He had always been civil, courteous, appropriate in his conduct. If his responses were brief, it was because brevity was efficient, not because he wished to silence her.

She was being dramatic. Women often were, in his experience.

He read on, his irritation mounting.

Today I spent four hours embroidering a cushion I do not want, for a chair no one sits in, in a room no one uses. This is what my life has become, the production of beautiful, useless things to fill beautiful, useless spaces.

I should not complain. Other women would envy me. I have leisure, comfort, security. I have everything except...

No. I will not write that word. It is ungrateful. It is improper. It is the complaint of a spoiled child who does not understand her own good fortune.

Alastair turned the page with more force than necessary.

Except what? he thought. *What could possibly be lacking?*

He had given her everything. A home. A title. Pin money and fine clothes and the respect of the neighborhood. What more did she imagine she was owed?

The entries continued in the same vein through the first year. Alastair skimmed them, his impatience growing. The same themes repeated, loneliness, invisibility, the sense of being observed but not seen.

He looked at me today, she wrote in one entry. *Actually looked at me, not through me, not past me, but at me. It lasted perhaps three seconds, and then his attention moved on. But for those three seconds, I felt as though I existed.*

Is it pathetic to treasure such a small thing? Probably. Almost certainly.

I treasured it anyway.

He set the journal down and pressed his fingers to the bridge of his nose.

When had he looked at her? He could not remember. But surely he had looked at her often, she was his wife, they shared meals, they attended events together. Of course he had looked at her.

But had he seen her?

The question was uncomfortable. He pushed it aside and continued reading.

The entry that stopped him was dated roughly eighteen months into their marriage.

I made a mistake today. A foolish one.

We had guests for dinner, the Ashworths and two other families from the neighborhood. The conversation turned to politics, as it often does when the men forget to guard their tongues around ladies. Sir Edward was holding forth about the reform bills, and I found myself, God help me, having an opinion.

I did not voice it. I am not so foolish as that. But I must have shown something in my expression, because Alastair glanced at me and said, quite mildly, "I trust the ladies will excuse our dull talk. Perhaps Mrs. Ashworth might prefer to discuss the new fashions from London?"

The conversation shifted. The moment passed. No one remarked upon it.

But I understood. I understood completely.

My opinions are not wanted. My thoughts are not welcome. I am to smile and nod and guide conversation toward safer waters. I am to be decorative, not substantive. Pleasant, not interesting.

I wonder sometimes what would happen if I simply said what I was thinking. If I spoke my mind, argued my positions, insisted on being treated as a person with ideas rather than a particularly elegant piece of furniture.

But I know the answer. Such behavior would be unbecoming. Unfeminine. It would embarrass my husband and shame my family. It would mark me as the wrong sort of woman, difficult, opinionated, unwilling to know her place.

So I stay silent. I keep my thoughts locked in this journal, where no one will ever read them. And I smile, and nod, and die a little more each day.

Alastair stared at the page.

He remembered that dinner. He remembered Sir Edward's tedious monologue about reform, and Mrs. Ashworth's equally tedious monologue about bonnets. He remembered being grateful when the evening ended.

But he did not remember Isobel's expression. He did not remember redirecting the conversation. He had not noticed, had never even suspected, that he had done anything to wound her.

I die a little more each day.

For the first time, his irritation began to curdle into something else.

He turned to the entries from the second year.

There was a letter from Charlotte today. She is to be presented at court next Season, and Mother is already fussing about gowns and connections. Charlotte writes that she is terrified, and also that she intends to be as much of a disappointment as possible, just to see Mother's face.

I laughed when I read that. Actually laughed, out loud, alone in my sitting room.

It has been so long since I laughed that the sound startled me.

I wonder what Alastair would think if he heard me laugh. Would he be pleased? Alarmed? Would he notice at all?

Probably not. He does not notice most things about me. I could dye my hair green and he would not remark upon it unless it affected his dinner arrangements.

That is unfair. I am being unkind.

But I am so tired of being kind. So tired of being grateful and pleasant and composed. So tired of performing contentment when all I feel is this howling emptiness.

Charlotte asked, in her letter, if I was happy. She asked it directly, which is very like her, no hedging, just the question itself.

I did not answer. I could not. What would I say?

"I live in a beautiful house with a handsome husband who has never struck me or cursed at me or treated me with anything less than perfect courtesy, and I want to scream every moment of every day"?

That is not a thing one writes in a letter. It is barely a thing one admits to oneself.

And yet it is true. God help me, it is true.

Alastair's hands were trembling. He set the journal down and stood, pacing to the window and back.

I want to scream every moment of every day.

This was not the mild dissatisfaction he had dismissed earlier. This was desperation, raw and terrible, hidden beneath a surface so smooth he had never thought to look beneath it.

He returned to the desk and picked up the journal again.

Today I asked Alastair about his childhood.

We were at dinner, in our usual places, with the usual twenty feet of mahogany between us. The silence had stretched long, and I could not bear it any longer, so I asked, just a simple question, the kind that invites conversation.

"What was your favorite game as a child?"

He looked at me as though I had asked him to explain the composition of the moon. A slight furrow in his brow. A moment of calculation, as though trying to determine why I might want such information.

"I cannot say I recall," he said finally. "I was not much given to games."

And that was all. He returned to his meal, and I returned to mine, and the silence stretched on.

I do not know why this particular exchange has lodged in my heart like a splinter. Perhaps because it was such a small thing, such a tiny overture, so easily answered. Most people could produce something, hoops, or tin soldiers, or racing through gardens. The question was not difficult.

But he could not, or would not, answer it. And he did not ask me the same in return.

He does not want to know me. That is the truth of it. He does not care what games I played, or what books I read, or what I dream about in the long hours of the night. These things do not interest him. I do not interest him.

I am not angry about this. That is the strange part. I think I ought to be angry. Instead, I am only tired. So very, very tired.

Alastair read this passage twice, three times.

He remembered the dinner. He remembered her question—odd, he had thought, out of nowhere, interrupting his thoughts about a dispute with the northern tenants.

He had not considered that she might be reaching out. That she might be trying, in her careful way, to build something between them.

He had simply answered and returned to his meal.

What games had she played as a child? He had no idea. He had never asked.

The entries grew darker as the second year progressed.

I have started timing the silences at dinner. It is a strange occupation, morbid, perhaps, but it gives me something to focus on besides the sound of cutlery.

Tonight, forty-seven minutes of silence, interrupted by three exchanges of fewer than ten words each.

I wonder if he notices. I wonder if the silence presses on him the way it presses on me, or if he finds it comfortable. Restful. The absence of demands.

Probably the latter. He seems perfectly content.

Then again, how would I know? I cannot read him. Three years of marriage, and I cannot tell you what pleases him or what angers him or what he fears in the dark of night. He is a closed book in a language I have never learned.

Perhaps I should make more effort. Perhaps if I tried harder, reached further, demanded more...

But I am so tired of trying. So tired of reaching across distances that never close. So tired of being the only one who seems to want anything other than efficient silence.

Maybe he is right. Maybe efficient silence is all marriage is meant to be.

Maybe I am the one who is broken.

The word broke hit Alastair like a physical blow.

Broken.

She had thought herself broken. Had believed that her loneliness was a deficiency in herself rather than a failure in him.

He thought of all the times she had been perfectly composed, perfectly pleasant, perfectly...

Perfectly invisible.

He had taken her composure as contentment. He had assumed that silence meant satisfaction. He had never, not once, considered that her stillness might be a kind of death.

The entries from the third year were the worst.

By now, Alastair was reading with a kind of horrified fascination, the way one might read an account of a disaster, knowing the outcome but unable to look away.

He is going to London. I did not ask why, and he did not offer. I do not know if he has a mistress there. I do not know if I would mind if he did.

He stopped. Read the passage again.

A mistress. She had thought he might have a mistress.

He did not. He never had. The trips to London were exactly what he said they were, business, pure and simple. There had been no women. There had been nothing improper.

But she had not known that. And he had never thought to tell her, because he had never imagined she might wonder.

Because he had never imagined that she wondered about anything.

I think perhaps I should mind, the entry continued. *I think a wife is meant to mind such things. But when I try to find the feeling, jealousy, or hurt, or even curiosity, there is nothing. Only this, a kind of blankness, where something else should be.*

I wonder sometimes if the fault is mine. If I am made wrong, somehow. Incomplete. Mother always said I was too quiet, too contained. She said men wanted warmth, and I had none to give.

Perhaps she was right.

Perhaps this is simply what I am.

Alastair set the journal down.

His chest felt tight, constricted, as if something were pressing against his ribs from the inside. His eyes were burning.

She thought the fault was hers. Three years of loneliness, of invisibility, of being treated as furniture rather than flesh, and she blamed herself.

She believed herself incapable of warmth. She believed herself broken, incomplete, fundamentally deficient.

And why would she not? What had he ever done to show her otherwise?

He forced himself to continue.

I received a letter from Charlotte today. She asked if I had found contentment in my marriage.

Contentment. Such a careful word. Not happiness, Charlotte is too clever for that. Just contentment. The bare minimum one might hope for.

I could not answer her directly. What would I say?

"I am content in the way a well-fed animal is content, warm, sheltered, undisturbed, without ever once feeling joy"?

That is not the sort of thing one puts in a letter.

Charlotte wrote of wanting to be seen, to be known. She spoke as if this were a reasonable thing to want, as if it were not greedy or improper to wish for more than shelter and provision.

I was taught that such wishes were dangerous. That a woman who wanted too much would always be disappointed. That gratitude was the highest virtue and dissatisfaction the greatest sin.

I have been grateful. I have been so careful to be grateful.

And yet.

And yet.

The words trailed off, incomplete, but Alastair understood what she had not written.

And yet it was killing her.

The final entries were dated just before her departure.

He was in the same room with me for ten minutes today. He was searching for a document, something about the tenant farms. He moved through the library, opening drawers, shifting books, completely absorbed in his task.

He never once looked at me.

I was sitting in my usual chair, not five feet from where he was searching. I watched him the entire time. I could have spoken. I could have of-

fered to help. But I wanted to see, needed to see, if he would notice me on his own.

He did not.

When I spoke up and suggested where the document was, he startled slightly. As if he had genuinely forgotten I was there.

I have been thinking about this moment all day. Such a small thing, ten minutes in a library, a husband preoccupied with work. It should not signify.

But it does. It signifies everything.

I am invisible. I have been invisible for three years. And I cannot...

The entry ended abruptly. A blot of ink marked the page, as if the pen had been set down suddenly.

Alastair turned to the next entry. The last one.

I have made my decision.

Tomorrow, after he leaves for Edinburgh, I will begin preparations. I do not know exactly where I will go or what I will do. But I know that I cannot stay here any longer. I cannot keep performing this role, playing this part, dying this slow and silent death.

If anyone ever reads this, if Alastair ever finds this journal and reads what I have written, I want him to understand. Not to forgive me, necessarily. Just to understand.

I am not leaving because he was cruel. He was never cruel.

I am leaving because kindness without attention is its own kind of cruelty. Because provision without presence is its own kind of neglect. Because I have spent three years waiting to be seen, and I cannot wait any longer.

I do not know if I will find what I am looking for. I do not know if what I am looking for even exists. But I would rather search for it, even if I fail, even if I starve, even if I die alone in some unfamiliar place, than spend another day in this beautiful house where no one knows my name.

Goodbye, Fenleigh.

Goodbye, Alastair.

Goodbye to the woman I was supposed to be.

Alastair closed the journal.

The candle had burned low, guttering in its holder. The room was very dark, very quiet. Beyond the window, the first grey light of dawn was beginning to touch the sky.

He did not know how long he had been reading. Hours, certainly. The better part of the night.

He sat motionless, the journal in his lap, and tried to reconcile what he had read with what he had believed.

He had thought himself a good husband. He had provided for her, protected her, given her everything a woman could reasonably want. He had treated her with courtesy, with respect, with the proper forms of attention.

And he had starved her.

Not of food or shelter, but of something more fundamental. The basic human need to be seen. To be known. To matter.

Kindness without attention is its own kind of cruelty.

Provision without presence is its own kind of neglect.

He had been so certain of his own decency. So confident that he was fulfilling his duties as a husband. He had never struck her. Never raised his voice. Never denied her anything material.

But he had denied her himself. His attention. His curiosity. His genuine interest in who she was.

He had treated her like a housekeeper with a title, a hostess with a wedding ring, and never once wondered what lay beneath the composed surface.

The journal slipped from his fingers and fell to the floor with a soft thud.

Alastair bent forward in his chair, his face in his hands, and wept.

He wept for the wife he had never known. For the woman who had died by inches in his house while he looked right through her. For the marriage that might have been something, if only he had bothered to try.

He wept for himself, for the man he had been, so certain of his own righteousness. For the years he could not reclaim. For the damage he did not know how to repair.

The dawn light strengthened. The candle sputtered and went out.

And Alastair, Duke of Fenleigh, sat alone in the darkness and finally, finally understood what he had lost.

Chapter Thirteen

In the days that followed his reading of the journal, Alastair was a changed man.

He did not know yet how deep the change went. He did not know if it would last. But something had shifted inside him, some fundamental understanding of himself and his marriage that could not be unshifted.

He had been blind. Willfully, catastrophically blind. And his wife had paid the price.

The first task, he decided, was to find her. Not to drag her back, not to force her return. But to speak to her. To tell her that he had finally, finally heard what she had been trying to say.

And to apologize. Though he suspected no apology would ever be enough.

He began with her family.

Letters went out to her father and mother in Hampshire, to her sister Charlotte in London. He wrote carefully, admitting that something was wrong without confessing the full scope of the disaster.

I am writing to inquire whether you have had any recent communication from Isobel. She departed Fenleigh some weeks ago, and I am concerned for her welfare.

The responses came within days.

Her father's letter was stiff with barely concealed irritation. He knew nothing, he said, of any change in his daughter's circumstances. If there was some difficulty in the marriage, it was hardly his concern. He had done his duty by arranging a suitable match; what happened afterward was between husband and wife.

Her mother's reply was more emotional, but no more helpful. She expressed shock and dismay at the news, demanded to know what had happened, and made clear that she expected Alastair to resolve the situation with all possible speed. The suggestion that her daughter might have simply left was, she wrote, "too scandalous to contemplate."

Neither of them knew where Isobel had gone. Neither of them, Alastair suspected, had ever really known their daughter at all.

Charlotte did not reply.

The silence from Charlotte was telling.

Alastair turned it over in his mind, examining it from every angle. Charlotte was Isobel's sister, her closest confidante. If anyone knew where Isobel had gone, it would be Charlotte. And if Charlotte was not responding, it was almost certainly because she had something to hide.

He could force the issue. Could travel to London, demand an audience, use the weight of his title to compel her to speak. But something in him recoiled from that approach. He had spent three years treating Isobel as a function rather than a person. He would not extend the same treatment to her sister.

Instead, he wrote again. A different kind of letter this time.

Miss Langthorne, he wrote,

I understand your reluctance to communicate with me. If you know where your sister is, you have every reason to protect that information. I do not write to demand answers or to threaten consequences.

I write to tell you that I have read your sister's journal.

I found it in a hidden compartment of her writing desk, and I read it. All of it. Every entry, from the first months of our marriage to the day she left.

I understand now what I failed to see. I understand what I did to her. And I am asking, not as her husband with legal rights, but as a man who has done wrong and wishes to make amends, that you tell me where she is.

I do not intend to force her return. I do not intend to invoke my authority or create scandal. I only want to speak with her. To tell her that I heard her. To apologize for everything I failed to give.

If you choose not to respond, I will accept that. I will continue to search on my own, and I may never find her. But I wanted you to know the truth of my intentions.

Whatever you decide, please believe this, I am not the same man who failed your sister. I am trying to become someone better.

Yours respectfully, Alastair Vane

He sent the letter and waited.

The reply came five days later.

It was short, written in a hand that trembled slightly, as if the writer had been uncertain whether to commit the words to paper.

Your Grace, Charlotte wrote,

I did not expect your letter. I did not expect the honesty in it. If you are lying, if this is some trick to draw my sister back to a life that was killing her, I will never forgive you.

But if you are telling the truth, if you have truly changed, then perhaps there is hope after all.

She is in Cornwall. A town called Trewarne on the southern coast. She is using another name; I do not know which one. But she is there, and as of her last letter, she was well.

I tell you this against my better judgment. Against her explicit request. But she deserves to know that someone finally heard her. Even if it is too late.

Do not make me regret this.

Charlotte Langthorne

Alastair read the letter three times. Then he folded it carefully and placed it in his breast pocket, next to his heart.

Cornwall. Trewarne. She was there.

He began to pack.

He chose to travel alone.

It was an unusual decision for a man of his station. Dukes did not travel without servants, without carriages bearing their crests, without all the trappings of rank and privilege that smoothed their way through the world.

But Alastair did not want to arrive in Trewarne as a duke. He did not want to arrive with the weight of his position pressing down on everything, reminding Isobel of all the expectations she had fled.

He wanted to arrive as a man. Nothing more, nothing less.

He hired a private carriage, plain and unmarked. He packed a small bag with simple clothes, the kind a prosperous tradesman might wear. He left instructions with Mrs. Harding for managing the household in his absence, and he set out on the road south without fanfare or announcement.

It was strange, traveling like this.

Alastair had not moved through the world without the buffer of his rank since he was a young man, before he inherited the title. He had forgotten what it felt like to be ordinary. To stay at inns where no one knew his name. To eat in common rooms alongside farmers and merchants. To be treated with indifference rather than deference.

He found, to his surprise, that he did not mind.

The discomfort was clarifying. Each jolting mile, each hard bed, each indifferent meal reminded him that he was doing something he had never done before, pursuing something that mattered with his own effort, his own hands.

He had always delegated difficulty. Problems were solved by servants, by secretaries, by the small army of employees who kept his estates running smoothly. When had he last faced an obstacle without the buffer of wealth and power to smooth his way?

He could not remember.

I am a function, not a person, Isobel had written. *A role, not a wife.*

Perhaps, he thought, he had been a function too. A duke. A landlord. A collection of responsibilities and expectations wrapped in expensive clothing. Not a person. Not truly.

If so, he was beginning to understand what that felt like.

On the second night of his journey, at an inn somewhere in Somerset, Alastair took out the journal.

He had brought it with him. Not as evidence or leverage, but because he could not bear to leave it behind. It was the most intimate record he had of who his wife truly was, and he found himself returning to it again and again, searching for clues he might have missed.

The entries he had skipped before, he read now. The small observations, the quiet moments of reflection, the glimpses of a mind far more active and engaged than he had ever suspected.

I have been reading a book of natural philosophy, she wrote in one entry. *It discusses how light can be bent and separated into colors by passing through a prism. I find myself wondering if people can be separated too. If the life we show the world is only one color of the full spectrum, with all the others hidden inside.*

What colors would I show, I wonder, if someone held a prism to my soul?

He remembered seeing her read. He had noted it without interest, another activity, another way she occupied her time. He had never asked what she was reading. He had never wondered about the thoughts that might be forming behind her composed expression.

There are so many things I want to discuss, she wrote in another entry. *Ideas I have encountered, questions I cannot answer on my own. But who would I discuss them with? My husband speaks to me of household matters. The ladies who call speak of nothing but gossip and children. There is no one who wants to know what I think.*

Perhaps I should not want anyone to know. Perhaps the wanting is the problem.

Alastair closed the journal and pressed his hand over his eyes.

Three years. Three years of living with a woman who thought about light and prisms and the hidden colors of the soul. Three years of dinners and mornings and thousands of small interactions, and he had never once asked her what she thought.

What had he been thinking? What had he been doing, all those hours and days, while his wife quietly starved for conversation?

He could not remember. That was the shameful truth. He could not remember what had seemed so important that he had not had time for her.

On the third day, the landscape began to change.

The rolling fields of the Midlands gave way to wilder, rougher country. The hills were steeper here, the sky larger, the air sharper with the smell of salt. He was approaching the sea.

He had never spent much time in Cornwall. His estates were in the north and east; he had no business interests in the southwest. But as the carriage wound through the narrow lanes, past stone walls and windswept moors, he began to understand why Isobel might have chosen this place.

It was as far from Lincolnshire as possible. As different from Fenleigh as one could imagine. A place of edges and weather and raw, unpolished beauty.

A place where a woman might reinvent herself.

He thought, as he traveled, about what he would say when he found her.

He rehearsed speeches in his mind. Apologies, explanations, promises of change. But each version seemed hollow, inadequate to the weight of what he had done.

What words could undo three years of blindness? What sentences could repair the damage of being treated as furniture rather than flesh?

He did not know. Perhaps there were no right words. Perhaps the only thing he could offer was his presence, his willingness to listen, his determination to be different.

And if she did not want to hear him? If she sent him away without a word?

He would accept that. He would have to accept it. He had no right to expect anything from her. He had forfeited that right through three years of accumulated neglect.

But he could not leave without trying. He owed her that much. He owed himself that much.

On the morning of the fourth day, Alastair reached Cornwall.

The sea appeared first as a distant gleam on the horizon, then as a vast grey presence dominating the landscape. He had the coachman stop at a high point on the road so he could look at it.

He had seen the sea before, of course. He had traveled to the Continent, had crossed the Channel more than once. But he had never really looked at it. Never stood still and let its immensity wash over him.

Now he did. He stood on the clifftop and watched the waves roll in, endless and eternal, and he thought about his wife.

He climbed back into the carriage and continued toward Trewarne.

The town was smaller than he expected.

It clung to the coast like a cluster of barnacles, grey stone buildings rising up from a small harbor where fishing boats bobbed at anchor. The main street was steep and narrow, paved with worn cobblestones. There were shops, a church, a few scattered houses, and everywhere the smell of salt and fish and sea air.

Alastair did not enter the town immediately.

He found a place on the hillside where he could see without being seen, and he sat down to think.

He had found her. Or rather, he had found where she was. Charlotte had said she was using another name, living a life he could not imagine. What would she be doing here, in this remote fishing village? Working in a shop? Taking in lodgers? Something else entirely?

He did not know. He could not know without looking.

But finding her location was not the same as knowing what to do next. If he simply appeared at her door, wherever that was, what would happen? She had asked him not to search for her. She had asked him to let her go. What right did he have to override her wishes, to impose his presence where it was not wanted?

He thought of Charlotte's warning, *If you are lying, if this is some trick to draw her back to a life that was killing her...*

He was not lying. He was not trying to trick her. But he also could not simply turn around and go home, pretending he had never come. He had traveled four days to reach this place. He had read her journal, faced the evidence of his own failure, committed himself to change.

And now he sat on a hillside above a Cornish fishing town, and he did not know what to do.

He watched the town for the rest of the afternoon.

He saw fishing boats come and go, their sails catching the autumn light. He saw women carrying baskets, children playing in the streets, the ordinary business of ordinary life unfolding below him.

And then, just as the sun was beginning to descend toward the horizon, he saw her.

She emerged from a shop on the main street, a basket over her arm, her head uncovered. She was wearing a plain dress he did not recognize, her hair pinned back in a simple style. She stopped to speak with a woman outside the bakery, and even from this distance, he could see her smile.

She was smiling. Laughing at something the other woman had said.

He had never seen her laugh like that. Not once, in three years of marriage.

Alastair watched her move down the street, watched her pause to pet a dog, watched her turn her face up toward the sun as if drinking in the light. She looked like a different person. Alive. Present. Real.

She looked happy.

The realization struck him like a blow. She was happy here. In this small town, living this simple life, she had found something she had never found with him.

And he had come to take it away.

No. He had not come to take anything. He had come to understand. To apologize. To offer her, if she would accept it, the chance for something different.

But watching her now, seeing the lightness in her step and the brightness in her face, he wondered if he had any right to disturb what she had built.

He stayed on the hillside until dark, thinking, watching, trying to decide.

In the morning, he would go down to the town.

In the morning, he would find her.

And whatever happened next would be her choice, not his.

Chapter Fourteen

In the end, Alastair entered the town without a plan.

He simply walked down the hill and into Trewarne's narrow streets, moving like any other traveler. Tired, road-worn, looking for an inn and a meal. He wore his plainest clothes, had not shaved in two days, and carried only a small bag. Nothing marked him as a duke. Nothing marked him as anyone at all.

The anonymity was strange. For his entire adult life, he had moved through the world with the weight of his title preceding him. Doors opened before he reached them. Servants appeared before he called. People looked at him and saw not a man but a position, a fortune, a name that had meant something for centuries.

Here, no one looked at him twice. He was just another stranger passing through.

He found a small inn near the harbor and secured a room for the night. The innkeeper was a jovial man with a red face and a curious manner, clearly eager to know what brought a stranger to their quiet corner of the world.

"Business in the area, sir?" he asked, as he handed over the key.

"Family matters," Alastair said vaguely. "I am looking for someone."

"Ah, well. Small town, Trewarne. Everyone knows everyone. Who is it you're seeking?"

Alastair hesitated. He could not very well ask for his wife by name, not when she was using an alias. And he did not want to draw attention to himself or his search.

"A woman," he said. "A relation. I was told she settled here some months ago."

"Ah, might be Mrs. Smith, then. She's the only newcomer I can think of. Came in autumn, works at Bakewell's Notions up the street." The innkeeper pointed. "Pretty thing, very polite. Keeps to herself mostly."

Mrs. Smith. Of course she would choose the most common name in England.

"Thank you," Alastair said. "That may be who I'm looking for."

He did not approach the shop that first day.

Instead, he watched. From his window at the inn, from a bench on the harbor wall, from the various vantage points he found as he walked the town's small streets. He watched the shop door open and close. He watched customers come and go, women mostly, carrying parcels wrapped in brown paper.

He did not see Isobel.

Perhaps she was inside, hidden from view. Perhaps she was elsewhere. He forced himself to be patient. He had waited three years without seeing her; he could wait a few hours more.

The afternoon wore on. The light changed, softening toward evening. And then, just before sunset, the door of the shop opened and she stepped out.

Alastair's breath stopped.

She looked different. The change was profound, though he struggled to articulate exactly what had shifted. Her dress was plainer than anything she had worn at Fenleigh, a simple grey cotton without ornamentation. Her hair was simpler too, pinned back in a practical knot without the elaborate arrangements that fashion demanded. She carried a basket over her arm and moved with a purpose, an energy, that he did not recognize.

But the greatest change was in her face.

At Fenleigh, her expression had always been composed. Pleasant. Carefully neutral. The mask he had mistaken for contentment. Here, walking down the street of this small coastal town, she looked alive. There was color in her cheeks that he did not remember. A quickness in her step that seemed entirely new.

She paused to speak with a woman outside the bakery, and he saw her face animate in a way he had never witnessed. A smile that reached her eyes. A laugh he had never heard.

She looked like someone who was happy.

The realization hit him like a blow to the chest.

This was what she looked like when she was not dying. This was who she had been all along, hidden beneath the composed surface he had never thought to look beneath.

He had done this. He had taken a woman capable of this brightness and dimmed her to a flicker. He had reduced her to silence and stillness and careful composure, and he had called it a good marriage.

She turned down a side street and disappeared from view.

Alastair remained where he was, his heart pounding, his mind racing. He had expected to find her diminished, perhaps. Struggling to survive in reduced circumstances. He had imagined himself swooping in to rescue her, to offer her the comfort and security she had left behind.

But she did not need rescuing. She was thriving.

The realization should have been a relief. His wife was safe, was well, was happier than he had ever seen her. But instead it felt like a condemnation. A testament to how thoroughly he had failed her.

She had needed to flee him in order to live.

He did not approach her that day.

He told himself he was being cautious. Strategic. He needed to understand her situation before he revealed himself. He needed to plan what he would say.

But the truth was simpler, he was afraid.

Afraid that she would refuse to speak to him. Afraid that the happiness he had seen in her face would drain away the moment she recognized him. Afraid that his presence would poison the new life she had built.

He thought of the journal, of all the entries that documented her slow suffocation in his house. He thought of the woman he had seen stepping out of the shop, bright, purposeful, undimmed.

Did he have the right to intrude on that?

On the second day, he watched her more closely.

He positioned himself on a bench across from the shop, a newspaper open on his lap as if he were simply a traveler enjoying the morning air. The shop opened at nine. Customers trickled in throughout the morning. And through the window, he caught glimpses of Isobel moving inside.

She was working.

The realization struck him with unexpected force. His wife, the Duchess of Fenleigh, was working in a shop. Serving customers.

Handling merchandise. Doing the kind of labor that women of her station never did.

And she looked, as far as he could tell, completely at ease.

At midday, she emerged with her basket and walked down toward the harbor. He followed at a distance, watching her stop at various stalls, selecting vegetables, haggling over fish, exchanging pleasantries with vendors who clearly knew her by name.

She was part of this community. In just a few months, she had become someone here. Not a duchess, not a function, but a person with a place in the world.

He watched her return to the shop, her basket full, her step light. And he felt something crack inside him.

This was who she could have been all along. This was who he had prevented her from becoming.

On the third day, he made a decision.

He would approach her. But not as her husband demanding her return. Not as a duke exercising his authority. He would approach her as a man who had done wrong and wished to acknowledge it.

Whatever happened after that would be her choice.

He waited until late afternoon, when the shop would be quiet, and walked across the street. The bell jingled as he pushed open the door.

The interior was small and cluttered, crammed with ribbons and lace and buttons and thread. An older woman stood behind the counter, grey-haired and sharp-eyed, with the weathered face of someone who had spent time outdoors. This must be Mrs. Bakewell, the woman who owned the shop.

Isobel was not in sight.

"May I help you, sir?" Mrs. Bakewell asked, studying him with frank assessment.

"I am looking for someone," Alastair said. His voice sounded strange to his own ears, rough, uncertain. "A woman. I believe she may be staying here."

Mrs. Bakewell's expression cooled immediately. Her posture shifted, becoming somehow larger, more protective.

"We don't take in women for that sort of thing."

"No, I did not mean..." He stopped, drew a breath. This was going badly. "Her name is Isobel. She is my wife."

The change in Mrs. Bakewell's demeanor was instant and alarming. Her eyes went hard, her jaw set, and she came around the counter with surprising speed for a woman of her years.

"I think you'd better leave, sir."

"Please. I only want to speak with her."

"And I'm telling you to leave." Mrs. Bakewell stopped directly in front of him, and despite being half his size, there was something in her bearing that made Alastair step back. "Whatever you think you're entitled to, whatever the law says about husbands and wives, you'll find none of it honored here. That woman came to me worn thin as paper, and I'll not have you wearing her thinner."

"I am not here to harm her."

"Harm takes many forms, sir. I've seen them all."

"I know." His voice cracked. "I know it does. And I know what form mine took. That is why I am here."

Mrs. Bakewell paused. Something in his tone had caught her attention.

"I read her journal," Alastair said. He had not planned to confess this, but the words came anyway. "She left it behind, hidden in her desk. And I read it. All of it. Every entry from the first months of our marriage until the day she left."

"And?"

"And I understand now. What I did. What I failed to do." He met her eyes, willing her to see his sincerity. "I never struck her. I never raised my voice. I thought that made me a good husband. But I was wrong. I was so profoundly, horribly wrong."

Mrs. Bakewell studied him for a long moment. Her expression did not soften, but something in her posture shifted slightly.

"She doesn't want to see you," she said.

"I know."

"She came here to escape. To build something new. She's been happier these past weeks than I suspect she's been in years."

"I saw her." Alastair's voice was barely above a whisper. "Yesterday, in the street. I saw her laughing."

"And what did that tell you?"

"That I never made her laugh. Not once, in three years of marriage. That I never saw her smile the way she smiled at that woman outside the bakery." He drew a ragged breath. "That I was so busy being a duke, being a landlord, being everything except a husband, that I never learned who she was."

Mrs. Bakewell was silent.

"I am not here to drag her home," Alastair continued. "I am not here to demand my rights or enforce my authority. I am here because she deserves to know that I heard her. That I finally, finally heard her. And that I am sorry."

"Pretty words."

"They are not only words. I have changed. I am changing. But I cannot prove that to you, or to her, in a single conversation. I can only ask for the chance to try."

The shop fell silent. Outside, gulls cried and the sea murmured against the harbor walls. The afternoon light slanted through the dusty windows, illuminating motes of dust that drifted in the air.

"She's not here," Mrs. Bakewell said finally. "She's gone to the market. Won't be back for another hour."

"I will wait."

"Not in my shop, you won't." But her tone had lost its sharp edge. "There's a bench by the harbor wall. You can wait there. I'll tell her you've come. What she does with that information is her own choice."

"Thank you."

"Don't thank me yet." Mrs. Bakewell's eyes were still hard, still watchful. "If you hurt her again, if I see even a shadow of the man she described in that journal of hers, I'll have you run out of this town on a rail. Duke or no duke."

"I understand."

"Do you?" She shook her head slowly. "I hope so, sir. For both your sakes."

Alastair found the bench she had described and sat down.

The harbor spread before him, boats bobbing gently at their moorings, the sea stretching grey and endless to the horizon. It was beautiful, in a stark, simple way. Nothing like the manicured grounds of Fenleigh, with their carefully planned vistas and ornamental features. This was raw. Real. Unpolished.

He understood why she had chosen this place. It was as different from her old life as possible. A complete break. A chance to become someone new.

He waited.

The sun moved across the sky. Fishermen came and went, mending nets, hauling catches, calling to one another in accents he could barely understand. Children played on the shingle beach. An old woman fed scraps to the gulls.

And still he waited.

He thought about what he would say when she came. He re-hearsed speeches in his mind, apologies, explanations, promises of change. But each one felt hollow, inadequate to the weight of what he had done.

Perhaps there were no right words. Perhaps the only thing he could offer was his presence. His willingness to hear whatever she wished to say.

The afternoon shadows lengthened.

And then, at last, he saw her.

She was walking along the harbor wall, her market basket over her arm, her head turned toward the sea. She had not seen him yet. She was simply walking, lost in her own thoughts, and there was something in her posture, a looseness, an ease, that he had never seen before.

She turned. Their eyes met.

And Isobel stopped.

For a long moment, neither of them moved.

Alastair watched the emotions flicker across her face. Shock, first. Then fear. Then something harder, more guarded.

She did not run. She did not cry out. She simply stood there, frozen, staring at him as if he were a ghost risen from the grave.

"Isobel," he said.

Her name. Just her name, in his familiar voice, and he saw her flinch as if he had struck her.

"How did you find me?" Her voice was steady, but he could see the tension in her shoulders, the way her hands gripped the handle of her basket.

"Your sister. I asked her to tell me, and she did." A pause. "I am sorry. I know you asked not to be followed."

"Then why did you come?"

The question hung in the air between them. The gulls cried overhead. The sea murmured against the stones.

"Because I read your journal," he said. "And I could not let you believe that no one heard."

She stared at him. He watched her process his words, saw the moment when understanding dawned.

"You read my journal," she repeated. Her voice was flat, expressionless.

"Yes."

"All of it?"

"All of it."

Something flickered across her face. Shame, perhaps. Or anger. He could not tell.

"That was private," she said.

"I know. I am not proud of having read it. But I found it, and I could not..." He stopped, searching for words. "I needed to understand why you left. And you had not told me. Not really. The letter you left said so little. And I was so confused."

"Confused?" The word came out sharp, edged with something that might have been bitter laughter. "You were confused?"

"Yes."

"I lived with you for three years." Her voice was rising now, the composure cracking. "I sat across from you at every meal. I managed your household, entertained your guests, performed every duty a wife is expected to perform. And when I left, you were confused?"

"I know how that sounds."

"Do you? Do you have any idea how that sounds?" She set down her basket, her hands trembling. "I wrote in that journal every night, Alastair. Every night for three years, I poured out everything I could not say aloud. And you, you didn't need to read a word of it to know I was unhappy. You only needed to look. You only needed to ask."

"I know."

"Then why didn't you?"

The question broke something open in him.

"Because I was a fool," he said. "Because I assumed that provision was enough. Because I thought that if you were not complaining, you must be content. Because I was raised to manage estates and obligations, not people. Not a wife."

She was silent for a long moment. The wind off the sea lifted strands of her hair, blowing them across her face. She did not push them back.

"Why are you really here?" she asked.

"To apologize." The words came quickly, as if he had been holding them back. "To tell you that I read what you wrote, and I understand now. What I did. What I failed to do. How I made you invisible."

"And then what? You expect me to come home? To pretend nothing happened?"

"No." He shook his head. "I expect nothing. I am asking for nothing. I only wanted you to know that I heard you. That your words broke something in me. And I will never be the same."

She stared at him.

The sun was sinking toward the horizon, painting the water in shades of gold and rose. Somewhere in the harbor, a fisherman was singing.

"I don't know how to believe you," she said finally. "You never saw me, Alastair. Not once, in three years. How am I supposed to believe you see me now?"

"You're not." His voice was quiet. "I have not earned that. I have not earned anything. All I can tell you is what is true, I was blind, and now I am not. I was asleep, and your leaving woke me. Whether you believe that, whether you can ever trust it, that is your choice. I will accept whatever you decide."

She was quiet for a long time. The waves lapped against the harbor stones. The gulls wheeled overhead.

"What happens now?" she asked.

"Whatever you want." He meant it. "If you want me to leave, I will leave. I will return to Fenleigh and tell everyone that you are visiting relatives. The scandal can be managed. Your reputation can be protected."

"And if I don't want to come back?"

The question cut deep, but he did not let himself flinch from it.

"Then I will find a way to live with that. I will tell whatever story is necessary to preserve your standing. I will not divorce you or abandon you or cut you off from resources. You are my wife. Whatever happens between us, I will honor that obligation."

She studied his face, searching for signs of deception. He met her gaze and let her look. He had nothing to hide anymore.

"I need time," she said finally. "I cannot make this decision now. There is too much to think about."

"Of course." He did not press, did not argue. "I am staying at the inn near the harbor. I will be there for as long as you need. And if you decide you do not wish to speak with me again, if you send word that I should go, I will respect that."

She nodded slowly. Then she picked up her basket and turned away.

"Isobel," he said.

She paused but did not turn back.

"I know I have no right to ask anything of you. But if you could find it in yourself to give me a chance, even a small one, I promise you this, I will spend the rest of my life trying to become the man you deserved from the beginning."

She stood very still. The wind caught her shawl, rippling it behind her like a banner.

"I'll think about it," she said.

And then she walked away, leaving him alone on the harbor wall with the sunset blazing around him and the sea whispering its endless song.

He stayed there until the stars came out.

He did not know what would happen next. He did not know if she would see him again, or send him away, or simply disappear into the life she had built without him.

But he had said what he came to say. He had offered what he had to offer.

The rest was up to her.

Chapter Fifteen

Isobel
 She did not sleep that night.

She lay in her narrow bed, staring at the ceiling, while her mind turned over and over like a wheel that would not stop. Alastair was here. Alastair had found her. Alastair had read her journal, every word of it, every shameful confession, every desperate thought she had poured onto those pages in the darkness of her chamber.

He knew everything now. Every hidden feeling, every suppressed complaint, every moment of despair she had never allowed herself to voice aloud. He had seen inside her in a way she had never intended anyone to see.

The exposure felt like a wound. Raw and tender and impossible to protect.

And yet.

And yet he had come. He had traveled four days to find her. He had sat on a harbor bench and waited, and when she appeared, he had not demanded or commanded or invoked his rights as her husband. He had apologized.

She did not know what to do with that. The Alastair she knew did not apologize. The Alastair she knew was certain of his own righteousness, secure in his position, untroubled by doubt. This man, this stranger on the harbor wall with reddened eyes and trembling hands, she did not recognize him at all.

Was it possible that people could change? Was it possible that three years of blindness could be cured by a few weeks of absence and the reading of a journal?

She wanted to believe it. That was the most frightening thing. Despite everything, despite the years of invisibility and the slow death of her spirit, she wanted to believe that he meant what he said.

But wanting was dangerous. Wanting had led her into this marriage in the first place, the wanting of security, of position, of a life that seemed stable and respectable. And look where that wanting had brought her.

She could not afford to want again. Not until she was certain.

When dawn finally came, grey and damp, Isobel rose and dressed and went downstairs.

Mrs. Bakewell was already in the kitchen, brewing tea. She looked up as Isobel entered, her sharp eyes taking in the dark circles, the pale cheeks, the evidence of a sleepless night.

"Sit down," she said. "You look like death."

"I feel like death." Isobel sank into a chair at the scrubbed table. "He is still here, I assume?"

"Saw him at the inn when I went out for milk. He was sitting at a table by the window, staring at nothing." Mrs. Bakewell poured two cups of tea and brought them to the table. "He didn't sleep either, by the look of him."

"Good." The word came out harder than she intended. "Let him know what it feels like."

"To lie awake all night, thinking about someone who isn't there?" Mrs. Bakewell raised an eyebrow. "I imagine he's had plenty of practice at that, these past weeks."

Isobel wrapped her hands around her teacup, drawing comfort from its warmth. "You think I should forgive him."

"I think nothing of the sort. What I think is that you should do whatever feels right to you. And if what feels right is sending him away and never seeing him again, then that's what you should do."

"But?"

"But nothing. There is no but." Mrs. Bakewell sat down across from her. "I told you once that courage is not the absence of fear but the decision that something else matters more. The same is true of forgiveness. It's not about forgetting what was done. It's about deciding whether holding onto the hurt serves you better than letting it go."

"And if I let it go and he hurts me again?"

"Then you leave again. You've done it once. You know you can survive it." Mrs. Bakewell's eyes were steady, unwavering. "But you'll never know what might have been if you don't give him the chance. That's the choice you have to make. Is the possibility of something better worth the risk of more pain?"

Isobel stared into her tea. The question echoed in her mind, unanswerable.

"I don't know," she said finally. "I don't know anything anymore."

"Then take your time figuring it out. He said he'd wait. Let him prove he means it."

Alastair

He had not expected to sleep, and he did not.

The room at the inn was small and plain, nothing like the chambers he was accustomed to. The bed was narrow, the mattress thin, the blankets scratchy with age. But it was not the discomfort that kept him awake. It was the memory of her face when she saw him. The shock, the fear, the guarded wariness that had replaced the brightness he had glimpsed earlier.

He had done that. He had put that expression on her face. Not through violence or cruelty, but through something almost worse. Through the slow, steady erosion of neglect.

He rose before dawn, dressed in the same clothes he had worn the day before, and went downstairs to the common room. The innkeeper was stirring the fire, preparing for the day's business. He looked up as Alastair appeared.

"Early riser, are you? Breakfast won't be ready for another hour, but I can get you some bread and cheese if you're hungry."

"Tea, please. Nothing else."

He took a seat by the window and watched the town come slowly to life. Fishermen heading down to their boats. Women emerging to fetch water or begin their daily errands. Children running in the streets, their voices high and bright in the morning air.

Somewhere out there, Isobel was waking too. Thinking about him, perhaps. Deciding what to do.

He did not know what he hoped for. Did he hope she would forgive him? Did he hope she would agree to try again? Part of him, the prideful part that still clung to the remnants of his old self, wanted her to come back. Wanted to restore the order of things, to undo the scandal, to return to the life he had always known.

But another part, a newer and more tentative part, wanted something different. Wanted her to choose what was best for her, even if that meant never seeing him again. Wanted her happiness, even at the cost of his own.

This was love, he realized. Not the duty and obligation he had mistaken for marriage. Not the comfortable arrangement of two lives running parallel. But this, the willingness to put another person's wellbeing above your own desires.

He had never felt it before. He was not sure he knew how to sustain it. But he was determined to try.

The morning passed slowly.

Alastair stayed at the inn, not wanting to crowd her, not wanting to seem as though he was watching or waiting. He ate breakfast without tasting it, drank tea that went cold in his cup, stared at the same page of a newspaper for an hour without absorbing a single word.

Around midday, a boy appeared at the inn with a message.

"For the gentleman staying here," the boy said, handing over a folded piece of paper. "From Mrs. Bakewell's shop."

Alastair's hands trembled as he broke the seal.

If you wish to speak further, I will be at the cliff path above the harbor at three o'clock. I make no promises. I only wish to talk.

Isobel

He read the note three times. Then he folded it carefully and placed it in his pocket.

She would see him. She was willing to talk.

It was not forgiveness. It was not reconciliation. But it was something. It was a beginning.

Isobel

She chose the cliff path deliberately.

It was a place she had come to love in her months in Trewarne, a narrow track that wound along the headland above the harbor, offering sweeping views of the sea. It was exposed and public, visible from the town below. Anyone watching would see two figures walking and talking, nothing more.

She needed that visibility. Needed the assurance that she could be seen, that she was not hidden away in some private place where anything might happen.

She arrived early, wanting time to compose herself. The afternoon was cool and bright, the sky a pale, washed blue. The wind off the sea was strong, whipping her hair around her face, tugging at her shawl. She stood at the edge of the path and looked out at the water, trying to quiet the clamor of her thoughts.

At precisely three o'clock, she heard footsteps behind her.

She turned. Alastair was climbing the path toward her, moving slowly, his eyes fixed on her face. He was wearing the same plain clothes as the day before, looking nothing like the duke she had married. Looking, instead, like an ordinary man. Tired and uncertain and very much alone.

"Thank you for agreeing to see me," he said, when he reached her.

"I agreed to talk. Nothing more."

"I understand."

They stood facing each other on the clifftop, the wind swirling around them. Below, the harbor glittered in the afternoon light. Above, gulls wheeled and cried.

"Walk with me," Isobel said. "I think better when I'm moving."

They walked in silence for the first few minutes.

The path was narrow enough that they had to proceed single file in places, then widened to allow them to walk side by side. Isobel set the pace, her stride purposeful, her eyes fixed on the track ahead.

"I have been thinking," she said finally, "about what you told me yesterday. About reading the journal. About understanding."

"Yes?"

"I want to believe you. I told Mrs. Bakewell as much this morning. But I don't know how." She stopped walking and turned to face him. "You were blind for three years, Alastair. Three years. And now you claim to see. How do I know this isn't temporary? How do I know you won't slip back into the old patterns the moment we return to Fenleigh?"

He was quiet for a moment. The wind ruffled his hair, and she noticed again how much grey was in it. He was not a young man. Neither of them were young anymore.

"You don't," he said finally. "You cannot know that. I cannot even know it myself." He met her eyes. "All I can tell you is what I intend. And what I intend is to be different. To see you. To ask questions and listen to answers. To be present in a way I never was before."

"Intentions are not the same as actions."

"No. They are not." He paused. "But I do not know how to offer you actions when you are here and I am there. I can only tell you what I will do if given the chance."

"And if I don't give you the chance? If I decide to stay here, to continue the life I've built?"

His jaw tightened. She could see the effort it took for him to keep his voice steady.

"Then I will honor that decision. As I said before."

"Even if it shames you? Even if there is scandal?"

"Even then."

She studied his face, searching for signs of deception. She found none. Only exhaustion, and sorrow.

Alastair

He had expected her to be angry.

He had prepared himself for rage, for accusations, for all the things she had never been able to say during their marriage. He had steeled himself to accept whatever she threw at him, knowing he deserved every word.

But this was not anger. This was something more complicated. She was assessing him, weighing him, trying to determine whether he was worth the risk.

It was, he realized, exactly what she should be doing. She had trusted him once, and he had failed her. She would not trust blindly again.

"I want to propose something," she said slowly.

"Yes?"

"I am not ready to return to Fenleigh. I am not ready to resume our marriage as if nothing happened. But I am not unwilling to know you." She hesitated, choosing her words. "To let you know me. If we could begin again, somehow. Not as husband and wife, but as something else."

"As what?"

"I don't know." She shook her head. "As two people who are trying to see each other clearly. For the first time."

The words struck him with unexpected force. Two people who are trying to see each other clearly. It was so simple, and so profound. It was everything their marriage had failed to be.

"I would like that," he said. "More than I can express."

"It would not be easy. I have three years of anger and hurt stored up inside me. I may not always be kind."

"I do not expect you to be kind. I expect you to be honest. That is all I ask."

She was quiet for a long moment. Then, slowly, she nodded.

"All right," she said. "We can try. But I set the terms. I decide how much and how fast. And if at any point I tell you to go, you go. Without argument, without appeal."

"Agreed."

"Then come back tomorrow. We can walk again. And we can see if this is something that can work."

It was not a promise. It was barely even a beginning. But it was more than he had dared hope for.

"Tomorrow," he said. "I will be here."

Isobel

She watched him walk back down the path toward the town.

He moved slowly, carefully, as if the ground beneath his feet might give way at any moment. She understood the feeling. Everything felt precarious now. Everything felt uncertain.

But beneath the uncertainty, something else was stirring. Something she had not felt in a very long time.

Hope.

She was not ready to trust it. Not yet. But she was willing to see where it led.

She turned back to the sea, watching the waves roll in beneath the cliffs. The sun was beginning to descend, casting long shadows across the water. In a few hours, it would be dark.

Tomorrow, she would see him again. Tomorrow, they would begin the slow, uncertain work of learning each other.

And perhaps, if they were very careful and very brave, they might find something worth saving in the wreckage of what they had been.

Or perhaps not. Perhaps this was all a mistake, a fool's errand, a path that would only lead to more pain.

But she would never know if she did not try.

She had spent three years being cautious, being safe, being everything that was expected of her. And it had nearly destroyed her.

Perhaps it was time to take a risk.

She pulled her shawl tighter against the wind and began the walk back to the shop.

Chapter Sixteen

Isobel
They met the next day, and the day after, and the day after that.

Each afternoon at three o'clock, Isobel climbed the cliff path and found Alastair waiting for her. Each afternoon, they walked together, sometimes for an hour, sometimes for two, while the sea crashed against the rocks below and the wind carried their words away.

At first, the conversations were awkward. Stilted. They spoke like strangers, circling around the things that mattered, afraid to venture too close to the wounds that still lay open between them.

"Tell me about your work," Alastair said on the second day. "At the shop."

"What do you want to know?"

"Everything. What you do. What you enjoy about it. What you find difficult."

She glanced at him, surprised. In three years of marriage, he had never asked about her activities with such apparent interest. He had acknowledged her management of the household in the way one might acknowledge the weather, a fact of existence, requiring no particular comment.

"I sort ribbons," she said slowly. "I serve customers. I help Mrs. Bakewell with the accounts."

"And you enjoy this?"

"I do." She paused, searching for words. "At Fenleigh, everything I did was about maintaining an image. Making sure the house looked perfect, that the guests were properly entertained, that nothing ever seemed out of place. There was no product at the end of it. Just an endless performance."

"And here?"

"Here, I can see what I've accomplished. A shelf I've organized. An account I've balanced. A customer who leaves with exactly what she needed." She smiled slightly. "It sounds small, I know. But it matters to me."

"It does not sound small," Alastair said quietly. "It sounds like purpose."

She looked at him then, really looked, and saw something in his face she had not expected. Understanding. Or at least the beginning of it.

"Yes," she said. "Purpose. That's exactly what it is."

On the fifth day, the weather turned.

Rain swept in from the sea, heavy and relentless, making the cliff path too dangerous to walk. Isobel stood at the window of the shop, watching the water stream down the glass, and wondered if Alastair would come anyway.

He did.

He appeared at three o'clock precisely, drenched and dripping, standing on the pavement outside the shop with his hat in his hands. Mrs. Bakewell took one look at him, muttered something about foolish men, and disappeared into the kitchen to make tea.

"You should not have come," Isobel said, but she was smiling. She could not help it. There was something absurd and touching about the sight of him, bedraggled as a drowned cat, refusing to let a storm keep him away.

"I said I would be here." He was shivering slightly, water pooling at his feet. "I did not want you to think I had given up."

"Come inside. Before you catch your death."

She led him into the kitchen, where the stove was warm and Mrs. Bakewell was already laying out cups and saucers. The older woman gave Alastair a long, assessing look, then handed him a towel.

"Dry off," she said. "And take a seat by the fire. You're no use to anyone if you fall ill."

"Thank you, Mrs. Bakewell."

"Don't thank me. Thank her for being soft-hearted enough to let you in."

They sat at the kitchen table, drinking tea while the rain drummed against the windows. It was the first time they had been indoors together since his arrival. The first time they had shared a space that was not the open, neutral ground of the clifftop.

"Tell me about your childhood," Alastair said.

The question surprised her. "Why?"

"Because I want to know. I want to know everything about you. All the things I never bothered to ask."

So she told him. About playing in the gardens of her father's house, inventing elaborate adventures with Charlotte. About the imaginary kingdoms they had built, the stories they had created. About her nurse, who had taught her to read, and the small sitting room that was the only place she had ever truly felt at home.

He listened without interrupting. And when she finished, he said, "Thank you."

"For what?"

"For trusting me with this. I know I have not earned it."

She looked at him across the table, at this man who was so different from the husband she had left. The same features, the same voice, but something fundamental had shifted. He was present now. Attentive. Real.

"You are earning it," she said quietly. "Day by day. Question by question."

Something flickered in his eyes. Hope, perhaps. Or gratitude. He did not speak, but he reached across the table and touched her hand, very briefly, before withdrawing.

It was the first time they had touched since his arrival.

Alastair

On the seventh day, he asked about the journal.

They were walking the cliff path again, the weather having cleared to a pale, watery sunshine. He had been thinking about how to raise the subject for days, knowing it was dangerous ground but knowing also that it could not be avoided forever.

"I want to ask you something," he said, "but I am afraid it may be painful."

"Ask."

"Your journal. The entries about feeling invisible. About wanting to be seen." He paused, choosing his words. "When did that begin? Was it always there, from the beginning of our marriage? Or did it develop over time?"

She was quiet for a long moment. The wind off the sea lifted her hair, and he watched her struggle with the question.

"It was always there," she said finally. "But it grew worse over time. At the beginning, I hoped things would improve. That we would learn to know each other. That closeness would develop naturally, as it does in marriages."

"But it didn't."

"No. The distance between us only grew. And the more it grew, the more I learned to hide. To present the surface you expected to see, and to keep everything else locked away."

"And I never noticed."

"No." She stopped walking and turned to face him. "You never noticed. You never asked. And after a while, I stopped believing that you could."

"And now?"

"Now I don't know." She shook her head. "You are asking. You are noticing. But I still don't know if this is temporary. A response to shock and guilt. Or something permanent."

"How can I show you that it's permanent?"

"I don't know." She began walking again, and after a moment, he fell into step beside her. "But I think we need more time. I think we need to keep talking, keep walking, keep learning each other. Until I can believe that this is real."

"As long as you need," he said. "I am not going anywhere."

Isobel

After Alastair left, Mrs. Bakewell fixed her with a knowing look.

"Well?"

"Well what?"

"Don't play coy with me. I saw the way you looked at him. The way he looked at you." She dried her hands on a towel. "Something's changed."

Isobel sank into a chair at the table. "I don't know what's changed. I only know that I'm starting to see him differently. He's not the man I left. Or perhaps he is the man I left, and I'm only now seeing who he could become."

"Those are two very different things."

"I know." She pressed her hands to her face. "I'm so confused, Mrs. Bakewell. Part of me wants to trust him. Part of me is terrified that if I do, I'll end up right back where I started."

"And what does your gut tell you?"

Isobel considered the question. Her gut. The instinct she had learned to suppress through years of conditioning, years of being told that her feelings did not matter.

"My gut tells me he's sincere," she said slowly. "That he genuinely wants to change. That if I give him the chance, he'll spend the rest of his life trying to prove it."

"And is that enough?"

"I don't know. I honestly don't know." She looked up at the older woman. "What would you do, in my place?"

Mrs. Bakewell was quiet for a long moment. Then she said, "I would give him one more chance. Not because he deserves it, but because you deserve to know if this is real. If it works, you'll have something worth having. If it doesn't, you'll have the closure you need to move on."

"And if it fails? If he hurts me again?"

"Then you come back here, and we drink a bottle of brandy, and we curse all men to the devil." Mrs. Bakewell smiled, a rare expression on her weathered face. "But I have a feeling it won't fail. I've been watching him these past two weeks. He's not pretending. He's genuinely lost without you. And a man that lost is either going to drown or learn to swim."

"You think he'll learn to swim?"

"I think he's already learning. The question is whether he can keep it up once the hard work starts."

Isobel sat with that for a moment. The hard work. The daily effort of being present, of paying attention, of treating another person as worthy of your time and care.

It was not something Alastair had ever done before. But perhaps, with practice, he could learn.

Perhaps they both could.

Chapter Seventeen

Alastair

Three weeks after his arrival in Trewarne, Alastair woke to a realization.

He was falling in love with his wife.

Not the comfortable affection of a long marriage. Not the dutiful regard he had mistaken for feeling in the early years. But something new. Something that had grown out of the conversations and walks and slow, patient work of learning who she truly was.

He loved the way she laughed when something amused her, the sound still rare enough to feel like a gift. He loved the sharpness of her mind, the way she argued a point with precision and passion. He loved the softness that emerged when she spoke of the things she cared about, the books and ideas and small pleasures that made up her inner world.

He loved her. The person she actually was, not the function she had performed.

The irony was not lost on him. It had taken three years of marriage and two months of separation for him to see what had been in front of him all along. He had been given a treasure and treated it as ordinary. Had been given a person and treated her as furniture.

Now, finally, he was beginning to understand what he had almost lost.

On the twenty-fifth day, Isobel asked him about his father.

They were walking the cliff path, the wind sharp with the promise of winter. She had been quiet for the first part of their walk, and he had let the silence sit, knowing by now that she would speak when she was ready.

"Tell me about your childhood," she said finally. "About what it was like, growing up as the heir to Fenleigh."

It was a question he had not expected. No one had asked him about his childhood in years. Decades, perhaps. It was simply assumed that he had been raised to his position, prepared for his responsibilities, molded into the duke he was expected to become.

"It was... regimented," he said slowly. "My father had very clear ideas about what a Vane should be. How he should conduct himself. What he should value and believe."

"And what were those ideas?"

"Duty above all else. Order, discipline, control. Emotions were weaknesses to be suppressed. Relationships were transactions to be managed." He paused, hearing himself as if from a distance. "I was not raised to be a person, Isobel. I was raised to be a function. A role. Just as I later treated you."

She was quiet for a moment. "You never told me any of this before."

"I never told anyone. It simply was what it was. I did not think to question it." He met her eyes. "Until you left. Until I read what you wrote about being a function rather than a person, and I recognized myself in your words."

"Recognized yourself?"

"I have spent my entire life performing a role. Being what was expected rather than what I felt. I thought that was strength. Now I wonder if it was just another kind of invisibility."

She reached out and took his hand. It was the first time she had initiated touch since his arrival. He felt the warmth of her fingers, the slight pressure of her grip, and something in his chest cracked open.

"Perhaps we were both invisible," she said quietly. "Perhaps we can learn to see each other now."

Isobel

That night, she could not stop thinking about what he had said. *I was not raised to be a person. I was raised to be a function.*

She had never considered Alastair's own experience of their marriage. She had been so consumed by her own pain, so focused on her own invisibility, that she had not thought about what his upbringing might have done to him.

He had been taught to suppress his emotions. Taught to manage relationships as transactions. Taught that duty and order were the highest virtues, and that anything softer was a weakness.

Of course he had not seen her. He had not been taught to look.

It did not excuse what he had done. Nothing could excuse three years of neglect. But it helped her understand. And understanding, she was beginning to realize, was the first step toward something else.

She lay in her narrow bed and thought about the life they might have had, if they had both been different. If he had been raised to value connection rather than control. If she had been raised to speak rather than submit.

They had both been shaped by forces beyond their control. Both been molded into roles that did not fit them. And both had spent their marriage performing those roles, never realizing that they were hiding from each other.

Perhaps, she thought, it was not too late. Perhaps they could learn to be different. Together.

Alastair

"I've been thinking," she said one afternoon, as they watched the sun sink toward the horizon.

"About what?"

"About what comes next. About whether I want to... to try again."

His heart stuttered. "And what have you concluded?"

"I want to go back," she said. "Not because I have to. Not because you want me to. But because I want to see if what we have here can survive at Fenleigh."

For a moment, he could not speak. The relief was overwhelming, crashing over him like a wave.

"You mean it?"

"I mean it. But I have conditions."

"Name them."

"This is not surrender." Her voice was firm. "This is not me giving up my freedom to return to a cage. It is a choice. My choice. And if that choice fails, if you slip back into old patterns, I will leave again. And I will not return."

"I understand."

"I need you to understand, truly understand. If we do this, everything has to be different. Not just conversations, but the whole shape of our life together. I cannot go back to being invisible."

"I would not ask you to." He took her hands in his. "I know I have not earned your trust. I know it will take years to repair what I have broken. But I will spend every one of those years trying. I give you my word."

She studied his face for a long moment. The wind gusted, and the light shifted, and in her eyes he saw something he had not dared hope for.

Belief. She believed him.

"All right," she said. "Then we'll try."

He brought her hands to his lips and kissed them, reverently, gratefully. "Thank you," he whispered. "Thank you for giving me this chance."

"Don't thank me yet." But there was warmth in her voice now, a softness that had been absent before. "We have a long way to go."

"I know. And I am ready to walk it. With you. For as long as it takes."

They left Trewarne on a cool, clear morning.

The town was just waking as they walked down to the harbor, where a carriage waited to take them north. Fishermen called out greetings; shopkeepers nodded from their doorways. Isobel had become part of this community, Alastair realized. She had made a life here, found a place where she belonged.

And now she was leaving it behind. For him.

The weight of that gift was almost more than he could bear.

"Are you ready?" he asked, as they stood beside the carriage.

"As ready as I'll ever be." She looked back at the town one last time. At the harbor, the cliffs, the shop where she had learned to be herself. "It feels strange, leaving."

"We can come back. To visit. To see Mrs. Bakewell."

"I know." She turned to face him. "But that's not what I mean. I mean it feels strange to be choosing this. To be walking back into a life I once fled."

"Are you having second thoughts?"

"No." She shook her head. "Not second thoughts. Just... awareness. Of what I'm risking. Of what we're both risking."

He took her hands in his. "I know the risk is greater for you. I know that you're trusting me with something precious. And I promise you, I will not betray that trust. Not again. Not ever."

She looked at him for a long moment. Then, slowly, she nodded.

"Let's go home," she said.

Home. The word struck him with unexpected force. Fenleigh had never felt like home to him. It had been a responsibility, an obligation, a monument to his family's legacy. But perhaps, with her beside him, it could become something more.

Perhaps they could make it a home together.

He helped her into the carriage, climbed in beside her, and gave the signal to the driver. The horses began to move, and Trewarne fell away behind them.

They were going back. They were going to try.

And whatever happened next, they would face it together.

The trip took 4 days until they reached Lincolnshire.

The landscape was familiar now, the flat fields and scattered villages of his home county. Alastair watched it pass through the carriage window and felt a strange mix of anticipation and dread.

Fenleigh was waiting. The house where he had been born, where he had lived his entire life, where he had failed so spectacularly at being a husband. He was returning to it now with the wife he had driven away, hoping to build something different.

Could they do it? Could they take the fragile thing they had constructed in Cornwall and transplant it to Lincolnshire soil?

He did not know. But he was determined to try.

"There it is," Isobel said quietly.

He followed her gaze. On the horizon, just visible through the bare winter trees, the pale stone walls of Fenleigh House caught the afternoon light.

"How do you feel?" he asked.

"Nervous." She was gripping the edge of her seat, her knuckles white. "Terrified, actually. The last time I saw that house, I was running away from it."

"And now you're running toward it."

"Not running. Walking. Deliberately." She turned to look at him. "There's a difference."

"I know." He reached over and took her hand. "And I will be beside you every step of the way."

The carriage turned onto the long drive, and Fenleigh rose before them. Grand and imposing and achingly familiar. Alastair felt the weight of it, the centuries of expectation embedded in those walls.

But he also felt something else. Something new.

Hope.

They were going to do this. They were going to try.

And perhaps, just perhaps, they would succeed.

Chapter Eighteen

I sobel
The house felt different.

She could not say precisely how. The rooms were the same, the furniture, the paintings, the careful arrangement of objects that spoke of generations of Vane wealth and taste. The servants were the same, with their careful deference and polished efficiency. Even the light was the same, falling through the windows in the patterns she remembered.

And yet.

Perhaps it was her who was different. Perhaps she was seeing Fenleigh with new eyes, the eyes of a woman who had lived simply, worked with her hands, learned to exist outside the structures that had once defined her.

Or perhaps Alastair's presence beside her was changing the experience. They entered together, his hand hovering near her elbow without quite touching, and she found herself acutely aware of him in a way she never had been before.

Mrs. Harding met them in the entrance hall. If the housekeeper was surprised to see the duchess returned, she gave no sign. Her face was its usual mask of professional composure.

"Your Grace," she said, inclining her head to Alastair. Then, with a smaller bow, "Your Grace."

"Thank you, Mrs. Harding." Isobel kept her voice steady. "I trust everything has been well in our absence?"

"The household has been maintained, Your Grace. Your rooms have been prepared."

Isobel glanced at Alastair. In the old days, she would have been escorted to her chambers, separate from his, on the opposite side of the house. But that was the old days. This was something new.

"I will take my things to the duke's chambers," she said. "Please have them sent there."

Mrs. Harding's eyebrows rose fractionally. It was the closest to surprise the woman had ever shown. "Of course, Your Grace."

When the housekeeper had withdrawn, Alastair turned to Isobel. "Are you certain? I do not want to presume anything. If you would prefer your own rooms…"

"I am certain." She met his eyes. "We are doing this differently now. That means being together. Not on opposite sides of the house, living parallel lives."

"Together," he repeated. The word seemed to glow when he said it. "Yes. I think I would like that very much."

Alastair

The first night back was strange.

They dined together in the small family dining room, not the great formal space where they had once sat twenty feet apart. The table was intimate, meant for four at most. They sat across from each other, close enough to speak without raising their voices, close enough to see the expressions on each other's faces.

"This feels strange," Isobel said, echoing his thoughts.

"Strange how?"

"I don't know exactly." She looked around the room, at the paneled walls and the family portraits, at the accumulated weight of centuries of tradition. "I suppose I expected to feel trapped again. Coming back here. But I don't."

"What do you feel?"

She considered the question. He watched her think, watched the small movements of her face as she sorted through her emotions.

"Cautious," she said finally. "Hopeful. Aware that everything depends on what we do next."

"Then let us do next things well." He reached across the table and took her hand. "What do you need? Right now, tonight. What would help you feel... safe here?"

She looked at their joined hands. Her fingers were rougher than they had been before Cornwall, callused from work. He found himself grateful for those calluses. They were proof of who she had become.

"Talk to me," she said. "Like we did in Trewarne. Like we've been doing. Don't let the house change us back into who we were."

"I promise."

"And tomorrow, ask me what I'm thinking. What I'm feeling. Don't assume. Ask."

"I will."

"And if you see me retreating. If you see me putting on the old mask, becoming the invisible duchess again. Tell me. Don't let me disappear."

His throat tightened. "I will not let you disappear. I swear it."

She squeezed his hand. "Then I think we might be all right."

Isobel

That first night, she slept in his chambers.

It was a deliberate choice, a statement of intent. They were going to share a life now, not just a house. That meant sharing space. Sharing intimacy. Learning to be together in all the ways they had failed to be before.

She lay beside him in the darkness, acutely aware of his presence. The sound of his breathing. The warmth of his body. The vast, strange newness of not being alone.

"Are you awake?" she whispered.

"Yes."

"I can't sleep either."

He turned toward her in the darkness. She could not see his face, but she could feel his attention, focused entirely on her.

"What are you thinking about?" he asked.

"Everything. Nothing. How strange it feels to be here again. How different everything is." She paused. "How different you are."

"Am I?"

"Yes." She reached out and found his hand in the darkness. "In Cornwall, I kept waiting for the mask to slip. For you to become the man I left. But it never happened."

"Because that man doesn't exist anymore." His voice was rough. "He died, I think, the night I read your journal. Something in me broke that night, and what rebuilt itself was someone different."

"Someone better?"

"I hope so. I am trying to be." He lifted her hand and pressed his lips to her palm. "I am trying, every day, to be worthy of the chance you've given me."

She felt tears prickling at her eyes. Not sad tears. Something else. Something she did not have a name for.

"I believe you," she said. "I didn't think I would, but I do."

They lay together in the darkness, hands clasped, breathing in unison. And for the first time in years, Fenleigh felt like something other than a prison.

It felt, against all odds, like the beginning of home.

Alastair

The first weeks were a careful dance.

They were learning new patterns, new ways of being with each other, and the process was neither smooth nor easy. There were moments when he forgot, when old habits surfaced and he found himself retreating into silence or preoccupation. There were moments when she withdrew, her face closing into the neutral mask he had once mistaken for contentment.

But they caught each other. Every time. When he saw her retreating, he asked her what was wrong. When she saw him distancing, she called him back.

"You're doing it again," she said one morning, when he had been staring at his correspondence for twenty minutes without speaking.

He looked up, startled. "Doing what?"

"Disappearing. Into your work. Into your head." She set down her book and came to stand beside his chair. "What's troubling you?"

He opened his mouth to say "nothing," the automatic response of a lifetime. Then he stopped himself.

"There's a problem with one of the tenant farms," he said instead. "A dispute over boundaries that's been festering for months. I've been trying to find a solution, but nothing seems to work."

"Tell me about it."

He stared at her. "You want to hear about tenant disputes?"

"I want to hear about what's occupying your thoughts. Whatever it is." She pulled up a chair beside him. "I managed a household for three years. I understand more about disputes and negotiations than you might expect."

So he told her. And she listened. And then, to his amazement, she offered a suggestion that he had not considered, a compromise that might satisfy both parties without requiring him to favor one over the other.

"That's... that's actually brilliant," he said.

"Don't sound so surprised." But she was smiling. "I told you. I'm not just decorative."

"No." He reached out and touched her face. "No, you are not."

Isobel

She began to share her reading with him.

Not just mentioning what she was studying, but actually discussing it. The natural philosophy texts she had loved for years, the poetry she had hidden like contraband, the novels that had been her only escape.

He listened. He asked questions. He tried to engage with ideas that were far outside his usual concerns.

"I don't understand half of what you're saying," he admitted one evening, after she had spent twenty minutes explaining a theory about the nature of light. "But I love watching you talk about it."

"Why?"

"Because you come alive." He was looking at her with an expression she was still learning to recognize. Wonder, perhaps. Or something deeper. "Your eyes light up. Your whole face changes. I never saw that before. Not once, in three years."

"You never asked before."

"I know." He reached across and took her hand. "But I'm asking now. And I will keep asking, every day, for as long as you'll let me."

She felt something shift in her chest. A softening. A letting go of something she had been holding onto for so long she had forgotten it was there.

"I love you," she said.

The words surprised her. She had not meant to say them. But there they were, hanging in the air between them, true and terrifying.

Alastair's hand tightened on hers. "I love you too," he said. "I think I have for a while now. But I was afraid to say it. Afraid I hadn't earned the right."

"Perhaps love isn't about earning rights." She turned her hand over, interlacing her fingers with his. "Perhaps it's about choosing each other. Every day. Even when it's hard."

"Then I choose you." His voice was rough with emotion. "Today and tomorrow and every day after that. For the rest of my life."

She leaned forward and kissed him. It was soft at first, tentative. Then deeper, more certain. A seal on the promise they were making.

When they parted, he was smiling. A real smile, the kind that transformed his face and made him look years younger.

"Come," he said. "Let's go for a walk. I want to show you the grounds."

"I've seen the grounds."

"Not with me. Not like this." He stood and offered her his hand. "Let me show you Fenleigh through new eyes."

She took his hand and let him lead her out into the fading afternoon light. And as they walked together through the gardens she had once thought of as a prison, she realized that something had changed.

The walls were still there. The expectations, the responsibilities, the weight of tradition. But they no longer felt like chains.

They felt, instead, like the framework of a life she was choosing to build.

With him. Together.

For the first time.

Chapter Nineteen

Alastair

Three months after Isobel's return, he made her laugh.

It was not intentional. They were in the library, their library now, a space they had come to share each evening. He was reading aloud from a letter he had received from a distant cousin regarding a land dispute that had been ongoing for three generations.

"And so," he said, setting down the letter with a sigh, "he concludes by informing me that the hedgerow in question is of utmost historical significance, as his great-grandfather once found a Roman coin near it."

"A Roman coin?" Isobel looked up from her book. "What does that have to do with property boundaries?"

"Nothing at all, as far as I can tell. But he seemed quite convinced it proved his point."

"Which was?"

"Honestly, I have no idea. I've read the letter three times and I still cannot determine what he actually wants me to do."

She laughed.

It was not the polite, careful laughter she had offered at dinner parties in the old days. This was something else entirely. A sound of genuine amusement, surprised out of her by the absurdity of the situation, and it transformed her face in ways that made his heart stop.

"I'm sorry," she said, composing herself. "That was not very dignified."

"No." He found himself smiling back, a real smile that stretched muscles he rarely used. "Please. Don't apologize. That is the most beautiful sound I have heard in months."

She went still. Color rose in her cheeks, a soft pink that made her look young and almost shy.

"You have never said anything like that to me before," she said quietly.

"I have never thought it before." He paused, considering. "No. That is not true. I must have thought it, at some point. But I never said it. I never let myself say it."

"Why not?"

He considered the question. It was the kind of question she asked now, probing, honest, requiring genuine reflection.

"Because I was afraid, I think. Of seeming sentimental. Of exposing myself." He met her eyes. "But I am learning that what I thought was strength was actually cowardice. And I am trying to be braver."

She was quiet for a long moment. Then she rose from her chair, crossed the room, and kissed him.

It was soft at first. Tentative. Then deeper, more searching, as if she was trying to tell him something that words could not express. When she pulled back, her eyes were bright.

"Thank you," she said. "For trying."

He reached up and touched her face, marveling at the softness of her skin, at the fact that she was allowing this, that she wanted this.

"Thank you," he said, "for letting me."

He was falling more deeply in love with his wife every day.

The realization no longer surprised him. It had become as natural as breathing, this constant discovery of new things to admire about her. Her sharp mind. Her quiet courage. Her capacity for forgiveness that still humbled him.

He loved the way she laughed when he said something absurd. He loved the way she argued with him about philosophy, defending her positions with passion and precision. He loved the way she looked at him now, as if she was actually seeing him, as if what she saw was worth looking at.

He had never felt this way before. Not during their courtship, not at their wedding, not in three years of marriage. He had felt duty, obligation, satisfaction in having secured an appropriate match.

He had never felt this.

But he still hesitated to speak of it too freely. The words "I love you" had been exchanged, yes. But there was more he wanted to say. More he wanted to show.

So he showed her instead. In every question he asked, every conversation he remembered, every small gesture of attention and care. He built his love brick by brick, day by day, hoping that when she looked back on this time, she would see a structure worth preserving.

Isobel

Four months after their return, she initiated intimacy.

It was not a momentous occasion in the usual sense. No candles, no special preparations, no careful staging of romance. They were simply lying together in the darkness, as they had done many nights before, and she found herself wanting more.

"Alastair," she said softly.

"Yes?"

"I think I am ready."

He went still beside her. "Ready for what?"

"For us. For all of it." She turned to face him, placing her hand on his chest. "I have been afraid. Of returning to what we had before. Of intimacy without connection. But this is not what we had before. And I want to know what it could be. With us. Now."

He was quiet for a long moment. She could feel his heart beating beneath her palm, faster than usual.

"Are you certain?" he asked.

"Yes."

"If you change your mind, at any moment, for any reason..."

"I will tell you. I promise."

He reached up and touched her face, his fingers tracing the curve of her cheek. "I want you to know," he said, "that I have never felt this way before. About anyone. Not even you, in the beginning. What we had then was duty. What we have now is something else entirely."

"What is it?"

"Love." The word came out rough, almost reverent. "Real love. The kind that sees and knows and chooses. I did not know it existed until I found it with you."

She kissed him. And this time, she did not stop.

Alastair

He had been with his wife before.

In the early months of their marriage, when duty required it and neither of them expected anything more. Those encounters had been brief, functional, devoid of any emotion beyond mild awkwardness. He had performed his role as he performed all his roles, competently, efficiently, without genuine engagement.

This was nothing like that.

This was slow and careful and tender. Every touch a question, every response an answer. He watched her face, learning what pleased her, adjusting, attending. He had never paid such attention to another person in his life.

And she was watching him too. Her eyes open, her gaze steady, seeing him as he had never been seen before.

Afterward, they lay tangled together, breathing hard, transformed.

"I did not know," she whispered.

"Nor did I."

"Is this what it is supposed to be like?"

"I think this is what it is like when two people actually see each other." He pulled her closer, pressing his lips to her hair. "I think this is what love makes possible."

She was quiet for a moment. Then she laughed, a soft, wondering sound.

"We wasted so much time," she said.

"Yes. We did." He could not deny it. Three years of emptiness that could have been filled with this. The thought was painful.

"But we have time now," she continued. "That is what matters. We have the rest of our lives to make up for it."

"Yes." He tightened his arms around her. "Yes, we do."

Chapter Twenty

Isobel Charlotte came to visit in the autumn.

She arrived in a flurry of luggage and chatter, full of news from London and eager to see for herself what had become of her sister. Isobel met her at the door, and they embraced for a long moment, holding each other tightly.

"Let me look at you," Charlotte said, stepping back to study her face. "Yes. Yes, it's true. You're different."

"Different how?"

"Alive." Charlotte's eyes were bright. "You look alive, Izzy. I don't think I've ever seen you look like this before."

They spent the first afternoon in the library, catching up on everything that had happened. Charlotte wanted to hear about Cornwall, about Mrs. Bakewell, about the journey back and the life Isobel was building now. She listened with rapt attention, interrupting only to ask questions or exclaim at particularly dramatic moments.

"And he really changed?" she asked, when Isobel had finished. "Truly changed?"

"He did. He is. It's not the same marriage, Charlotte. It's something entirely new."

"I can see that." Charlotte glanced toward the door, where Alastair's voice could be heard in the corridor, giving instructions to a servant. "He's different with you. The way he looks at you, the way he listens when you speak. It's like you're the most important person in the world."

"I think, to him, I am." Isobel smiled. "I never thought I would say that. But I think it's true."

"Then I'm glad." Charlotte reached out and took her hand. "You deserve this, Izzy. After everything. You deserve to be happy."

"So do you." Isobel squeezed her hand. "When are you going to find someone who sees you the way Alastair sees me?"

Charlotte laughed. "When I find someone who isn't a boiled turnip, I'll let you know."

Alastair

He found them in the garden the next day, walking arm in arm through the autumn leaves.

Charlotte looked up as he approached, her expression assessing. She had been watching him carefully since her arrival, evaluating, judging. He did not blame her. She had every right to be skeptical.

"Might I join you?" he asked.

"Of course." Isobel smiled and extended her hand. "We were just talking about the winter plans. Charlotte has some ideas about the Christmas ball."

"Oh?" He fell into step beside them. "What sort of ideas?"

Charlotte launched into an enthusiastic description of decorations and music and guest lists. Alastair listened carefully, asking questions, offering suggestions. He saw the surprise in Charlotte's eyes, the gradual softening of her skepticism.

"You're actually interested," she said finally. "In party planning."

"I am interested in anything that matters to the people I love." He glanced at Isobel. "And this clearly matters to you."

"It does." Isobel's voice was warm. "Charlotte has wonderful taste."

"Then we shall put her in charge. Charlotte, you have carte blanche. Whatever you need, whatever you want. Make it memorable."

Charlotte stared at him. Then she laughed, a bright, delighted sound.

"I take it back," she said to Isobel. "He's not so bad after all."

"I told you." Isobel leaned her head against his shoulder. "He just needed time to learn."

Isobel

The Christmas ball was a triumph.

Charlotte had outdone herself, the great hall decorated with evergreen and candlelight, the music lively and elegant, the guests charmed by the warmth and welcome of their hosts. But the true triumph, Isobel thought, was not the decorations or the music.

It was her.

She moved through the evening with a confidence she had never felt before. Not the brittle composure of her early years as duchess, the careful performance that had hidden her emptiness. This was something different. Something real.

She was herself. Fully, completely, unapologetically herself. And for the first time in her life, that felt like enough.

"You're radiant tonight," Alastair said, as they took the floor for the first dance.

"I feel radiant." She smiled up at him. "I feel like I belong here. Not because I have to, but because I want to."

"That is all I ever wanted for you."

"I know." She rested her head against his shoulder as they moved through the dance. "I know that now."

The music swelled around them, and for a moment, nothing existed but this, the two of them, moving together, perfectly in sync. The room faded away. The guests faded away. There was only Alastair, and her, and the life they had built from the ruins of what came before.

"I love you," she whispered.

"I love you too." He held her closer. "Forever."

Chapter Twenty-One

Three Years Later
Isobel

The nursery at Fenleigh faced west, catching the golden light of late afternoon.

Isobel stood at the window, watching the sun sink toward the horizon, while behind her the baby slept in her cradle. Eleanor Rose Vane, three months old, with her father's dark hair and her mother's grey eyes. A small miracle, unexpected and profoundly wanted.

The pregnancy had not been planned. After three years of their first marriage without conception, and then the months of separation and rebuilding, Isobel had assumed that children were not in their future. She had made her peace with it, found other forms of meaning and purpose.

And then, just over a year after her return, the signs had appeared.

She remembered the moment she had told Alastair. His face, transformed by wonder. His hands, trembling as they reached for her. His voice, rough with emotion, "A child. Our child."

"Yes," she had said. "Ours."

The pregnancy had been smooth, the birth uneventful, and now their daughter lay sleeping, tiny fists curled, chest rising and falling with each soft breath. Isobel watched her and felt something she could not quite name. Gratitude, perhaps. Or awe. Or simply love, in its purest and most uncomplicated form.

This child would never know what her parents had been before. Would never know about the years of silence, the months of separation, the painful rebuilding of a marriage that had been broken almost beyond repair. She would know only this, that her mother and father loved each other, and loved her, and were present and attentive and real.

It was, Isobel thought, the greatest gift they could give her.

She heard footsteps in the corridor and turned as Alastair entered the room.

He moved quietly, as he always did near the nursery, and came to stand beside her at the window. Together, they looked down at their sleeping daughter.

"She has your nose," Isobel said.

"Poor thing."

"I like your nose." She smiled. "I like all of you, actually. Even the parts that took some time to appreciate."

"High praise indeed." He put his arm around her waist, drawing her close. "How are you feeling?"

"Tired. Happy. Overwhelmed." She leaned into him. "I never imagined this. Any of this. Not the baby, not us, not the life we've built."

"Nor did I." He pressed a kiss to her temple. "And yet here we are."

"Here we are."

They stood together in the fading light, watching their daughter sleep, and the silence between them was not empty. It was full. Full of everything they had been through, everything they had become, everything they would continue to become in the years ahead.

Alastair

He had not known it was possible to love like this.

Not just Isobel, though he loved her more than ever. But Eleanor. This small, helpless creature who had entered their lives and rearranged everything around her. He had thought he understood love after reconciling with Isobel. He had been wrong.

This was different. This was vast and terrifying and wonderful, all at once.

"She has your eyes," he said, looking down at the sleeping baby.

"Does she?"

"The color. And the expression. That particular way of looking at the world, as if you're seeing more than anyone else."

Isobel laughed softly. "She's three months old. I don't think she's seeing much of anything yet."

"She will." He touched the baby's cheek, marveling at its softness. "She will see everything. And we will teach her how to look."

"What will we teach her?"

"To be curious. To be kind. To see people as people, not functions." He met Isobel's eyes. "To love with her eyes open."

She reached up and touched his face. "You have learned so much."

"I had a good teacher."

"We taught each other." She smiled. "We're still teaching each other."

Eleanor stirred in her cradle, making small sounds of a baby waking. Isobel moved to pick her up, settling her against her shoulder, and Alastair watched them together, his wife, his daughter, the center of his world.

Isobel

Later that evening, when Eleanor had been fed and settled for the night, Isobel and Alastair walked in the gardens.

The spring evening was cool and clear, the sky deepening from blue to purple as the stars began to appear. They walked slowly, arm in arm, not speaking, simply being together.

"I have been thinking," Isobel said finally, "about the woman I was when I first came to Fenleigh."

"Oh?"

"She seems like a stranger now. Someone I knew once, long ago, but cannot quite remember." She paused, searching for words. "I was so afraid then. So small. I had compressed myself into the space I thought I was allowed, and I did not even know I had done it."

"I did not help with that."

"No. You did not." She said it without accusation. It was simply fact, acknowledged and set aside. "But I am not that woman anymore. And you are not that man. We have both become someone new."

"Together."

"Yes. Together." She stopped walking and turned to face him. "I want to tell you something. Something I have never said before."

"Tell me."

"I am happy." The words came out simple, unadorned. "Not just content. Not just satisfied. Happy. Genuinely, deeply, entirely happy. And I did not know that was possible for me. I thought happiness was something other people felt, not something I was capable of."

"And now?"

"Now I know differently. You have taught me differently." She took his face in her hands. "I love you, Alastair. Not despite what we were, but because of what we have become. Not in spite of the pain, but through it. This love, the love we have now, is something precious. Something earned. And I would not trade it for anything."

He kissed her then, there in the garden, with the stars coming out overhead and the spring air soft around them. And when they parted, his eyes were bright.

"I love you too," he said. "More than I have words to express. You are my wife, my partner, my dearest friend. You are the mother of my child. You are everything."

"As are you."

www.ingramcontent.com/pod-product-compliance
Lightning Source LLC
Chambersburg PA
CBHW071157180726
48291CB00007B/2500